WELCOME TO
PASSPORT TO READING
A beginning reader's ticket to a brand-new world!

Every book in this program is designed to build read-along and read-alone skills, level by level, through engaging and enriching stories. As the reader turns each page, he or she will become more confident with new vocabulary, sight words, and comprehension.

These PASSPORT TO READING levels will help you choose the perfect book for every reader.

READING TOGETHER
Read short words in simple sentence structures together to begin a reader's journey.

READING OUT LOUD
Encourage developing readers to sound out words in more complex stories with simple vocabulary.

READING INDEPENDENTLY
Newly independent readers gain confidence reading more complex sentences with higher word counts.

READY TO READ MORE
Readers prepare for chapter books with fewer illustrations and longer paragraphs.

This book features sight words from the educator-supported Dolch Sight Words List. This encourages the reader to recognize commonly used vocabulary words, increasing reading speed and fluency.

Enjoy the journey!

ABDOPUBLISHING.COM

Reinforced library bound edition published in 2018 by Spotlight, a division of ABDO, PO Box 398166, Minneapolis, Minnesota 55439. Spotlight produces high-quality reinforced library bound editions for schools and libraries. Published by agreement with Little, Brown and Company.

Printed in the United States of America, North Mankato, Minnesota.
092017
012018

THIS BOOK CONTAINS RECYCLED MATERIALS

Licensed By:

LITTLE, BROWN

Little, Brown and Company

Hachette Book Group, 1290 Avenue of the Americas, New York, NY 10104

Little, Brown and Company is a division of Hachette Book Group, Inc.
The Little, Brown name and logo are trademarks of Hachette Book Group, Inc.

LIBRARY OF CONGRESS CATALOGING-IN-PUBLICATION DATA

This book was previously cataloged with the following information:

Fox, Jennifer.
Hearts and hooves / adapted by Jennifer Fox ; based on the episode "Hearts and Hooves Day" written by Meghan McCarthy. — First edition.
pages cm. — (My little pony) (Passport to reading. Level 1)
ISBN 978-0-316-24797-9
I. McCarthy, Meghan. Hearts and hooves day. II. Title.
PZ7.F85927He 2014
[E]—dc23
2013007282

978-1-5321-4091-4 (Reinforced Library Bound Edition)

Spotlight

A Division of ABDO
abdopublishing.com

my LITTLE PONY

HEARTS AND HOOVES

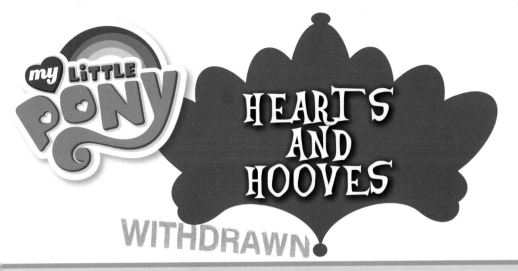

Adapted by **Jennifer Fox**

Based on the episode "Hearts and Hooves Day"

written by **Meghan McCarthy**

LB
LITTLE, BROWN AND COMPANY
New York Boston

ABDO
Spotlight

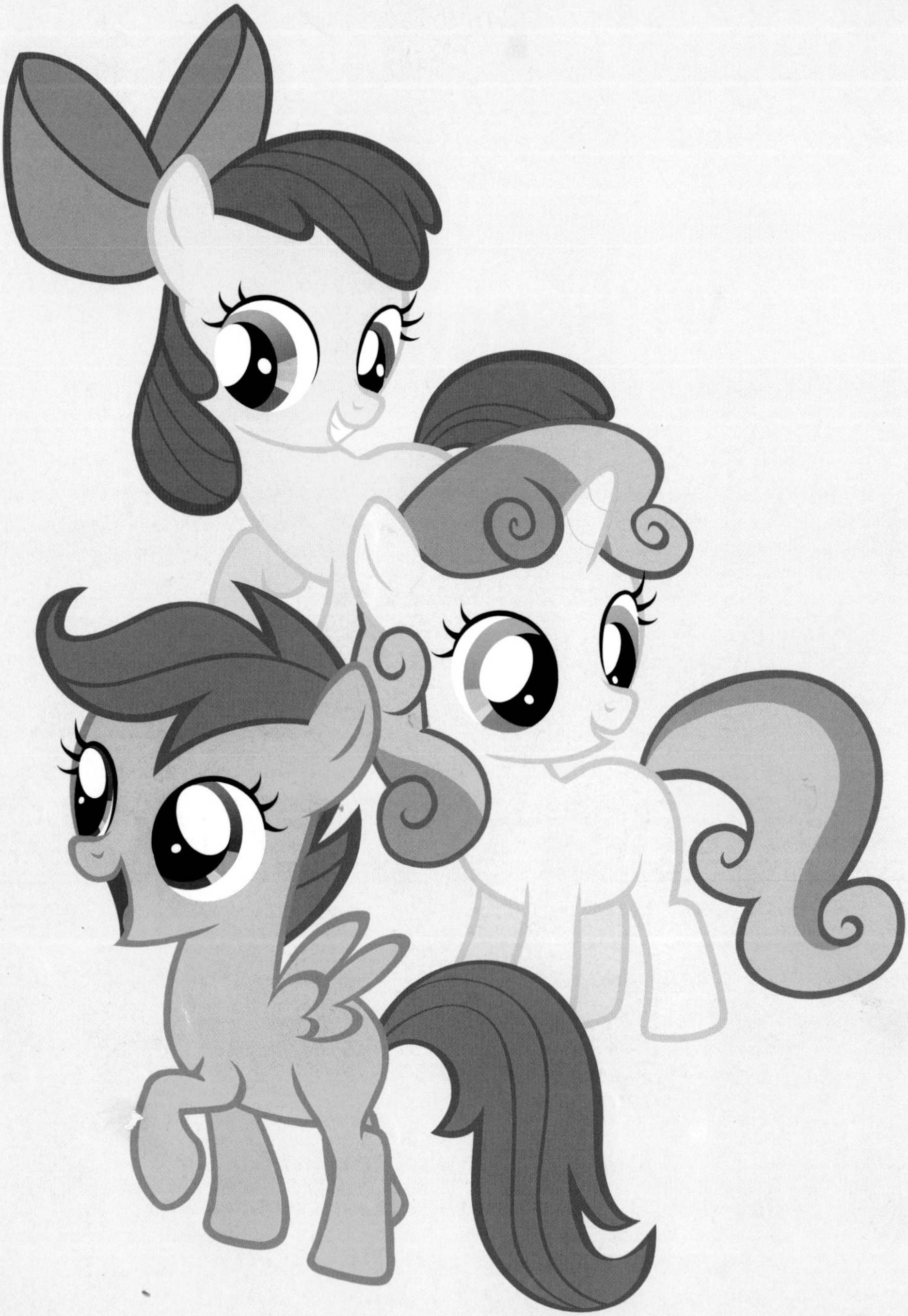

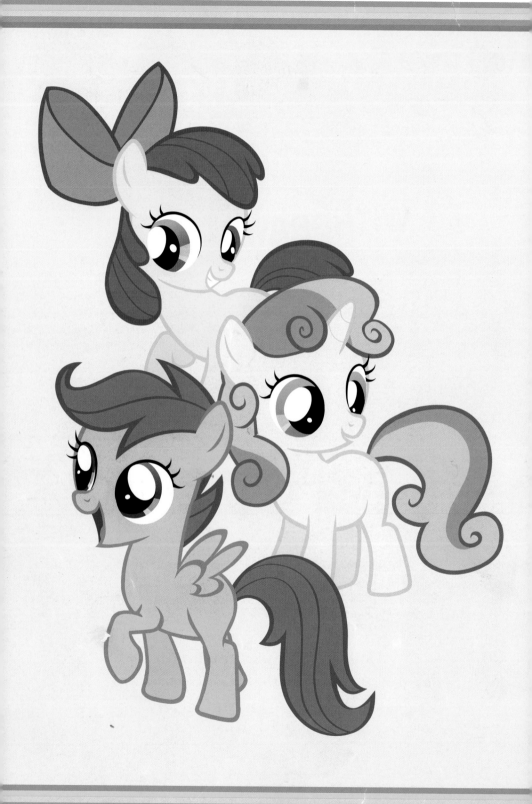

Attention, My Little Pony fans!
Look for these items when you read this book.
Can you spot them all?

valentine

smelly

picnic

potion

The Cutie Mark Crusaders are making a valentine for their favorite teacher, Miss Cheerilee.

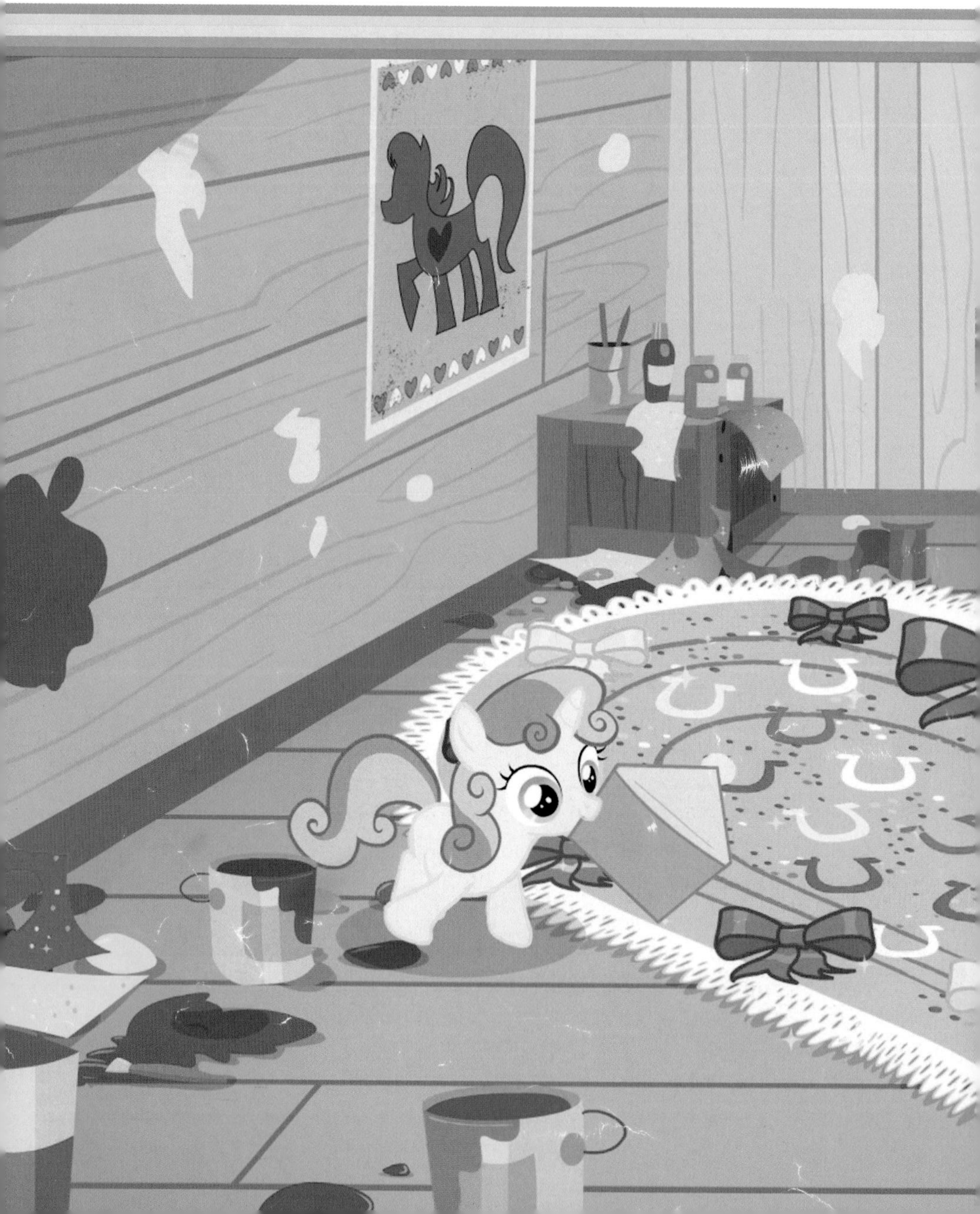

“More lace!” says Sweetie Belle.

“More hoof prints!” says Apple Bloom.

“More glitter!” says Scootaloo.

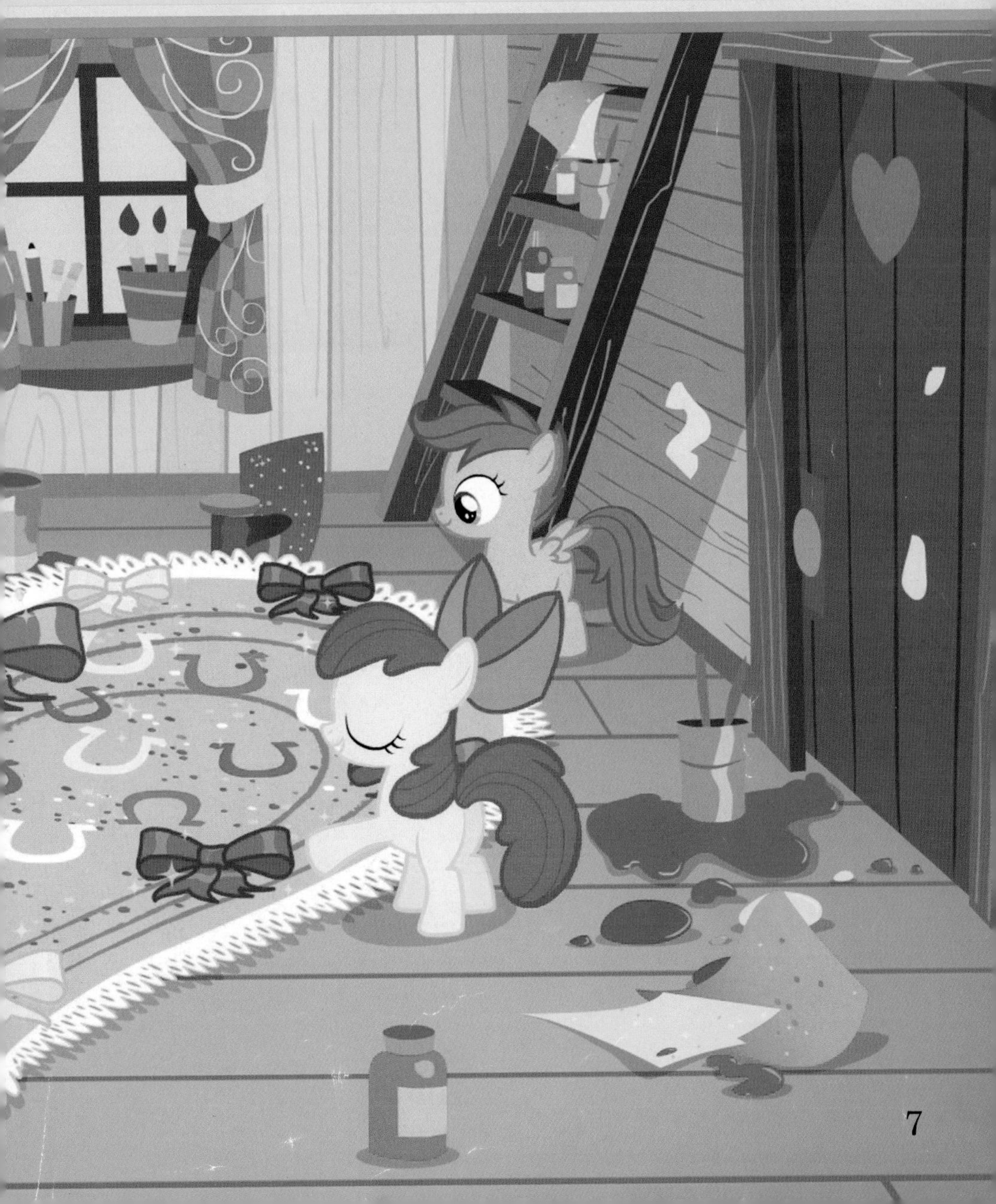

Hearts and Hooves Day
only comes once a year.

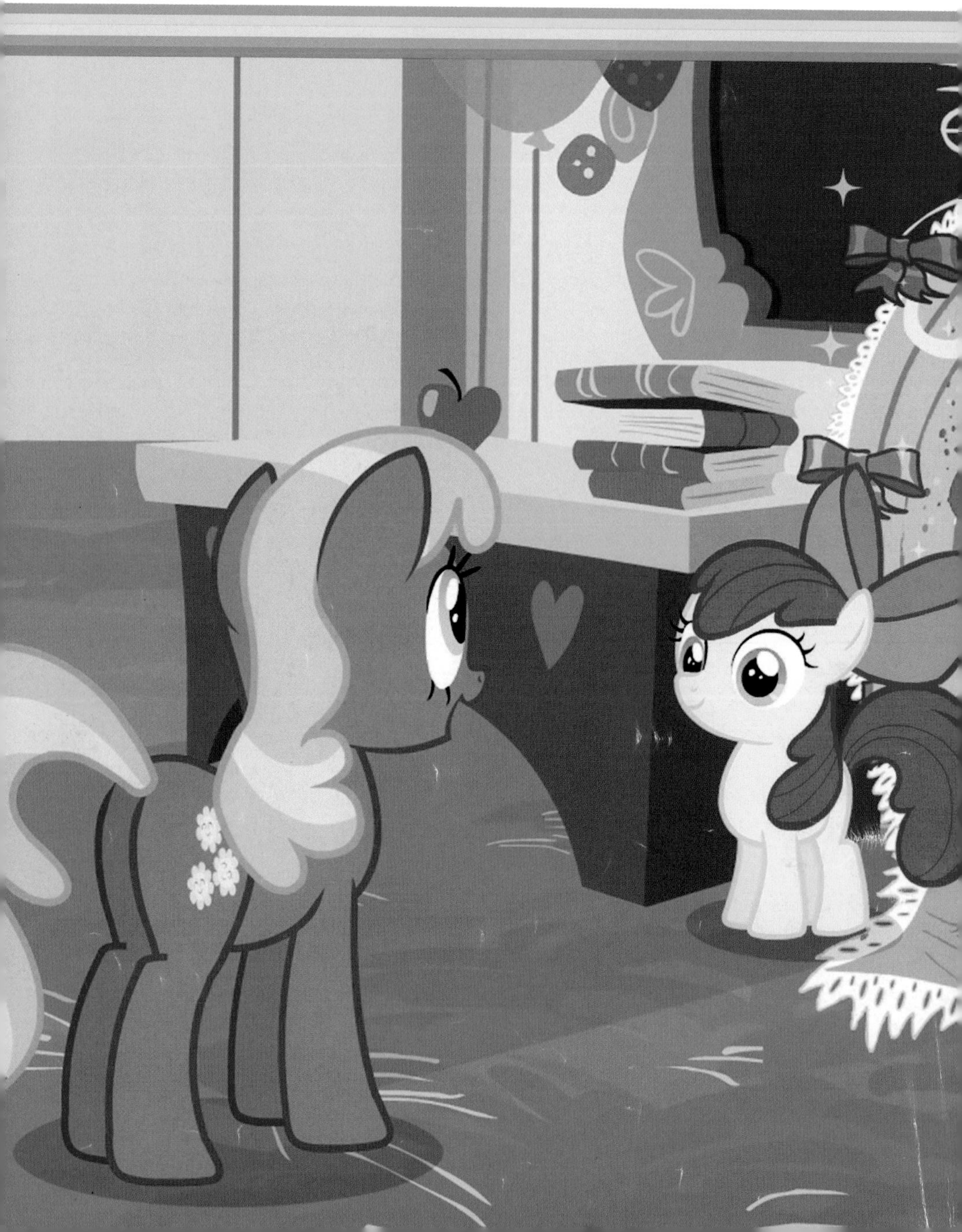

They want Miss Cheerilee to have
the best one ever!
The ponies give their teacher the valentine.

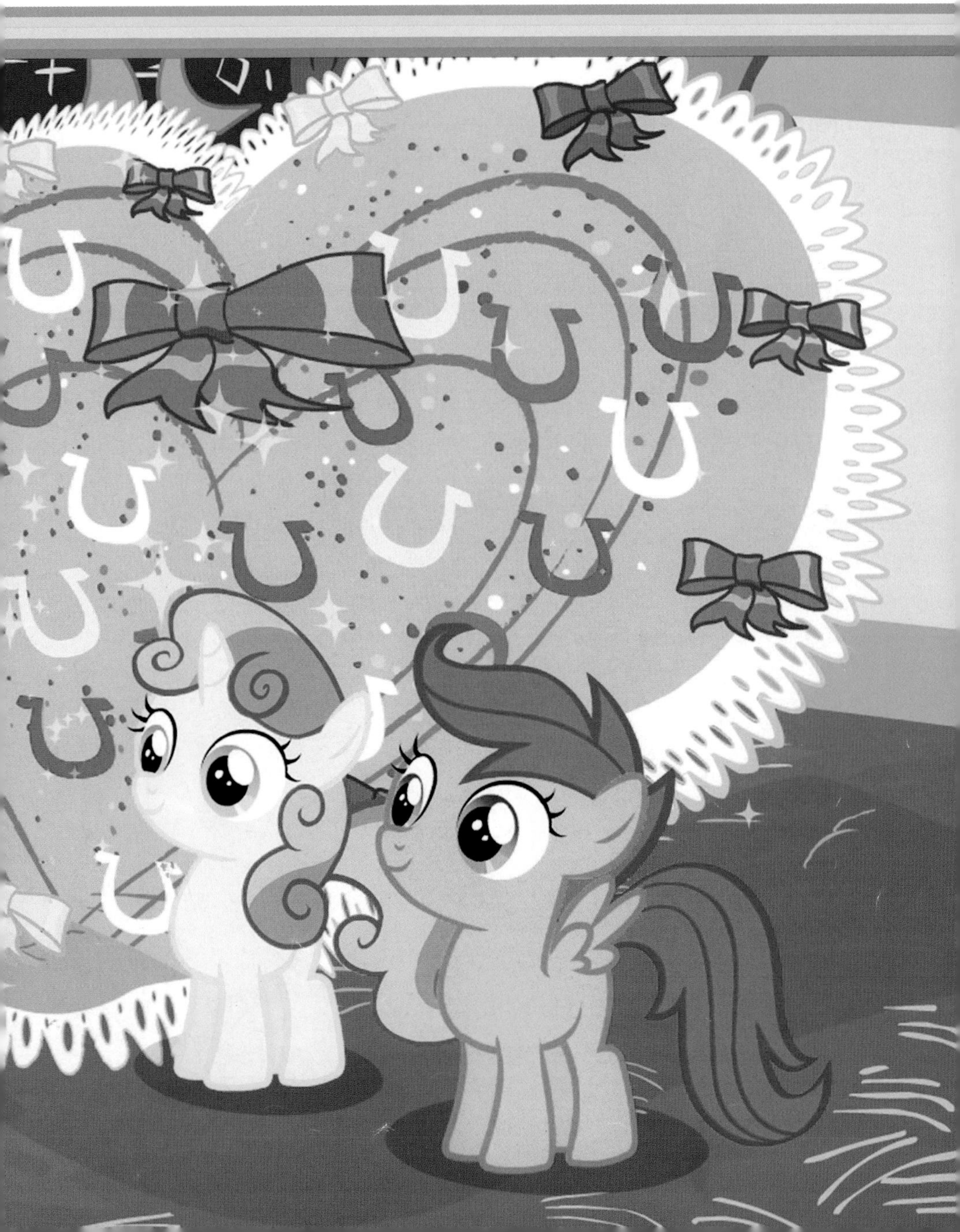

“Do you have a very
special somepony?”
Sweetie Belle asks Miss Cheerilee.

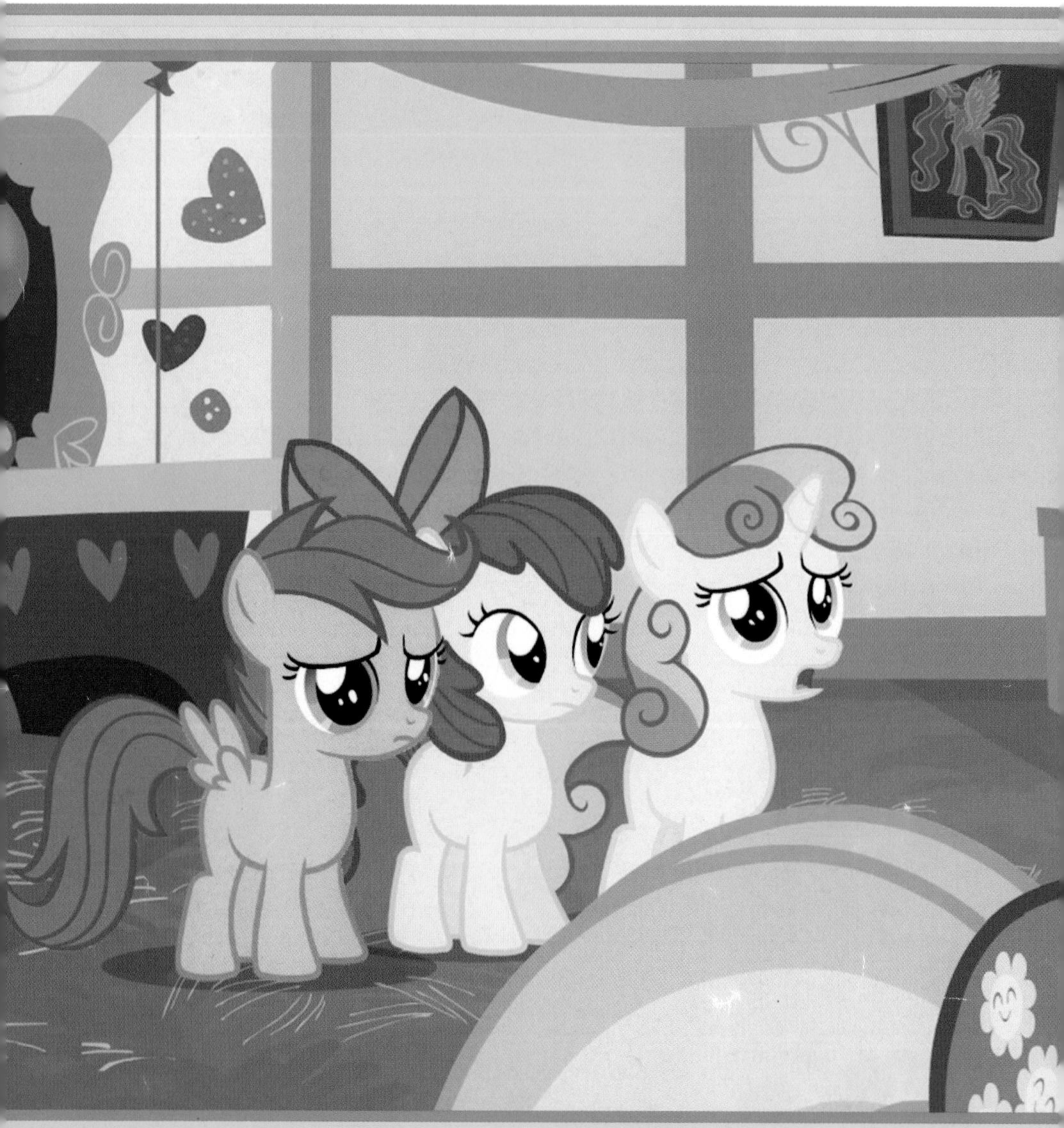

"No," Miss Cheerilee says.

The Cutie Mark Crusaders get an idea!

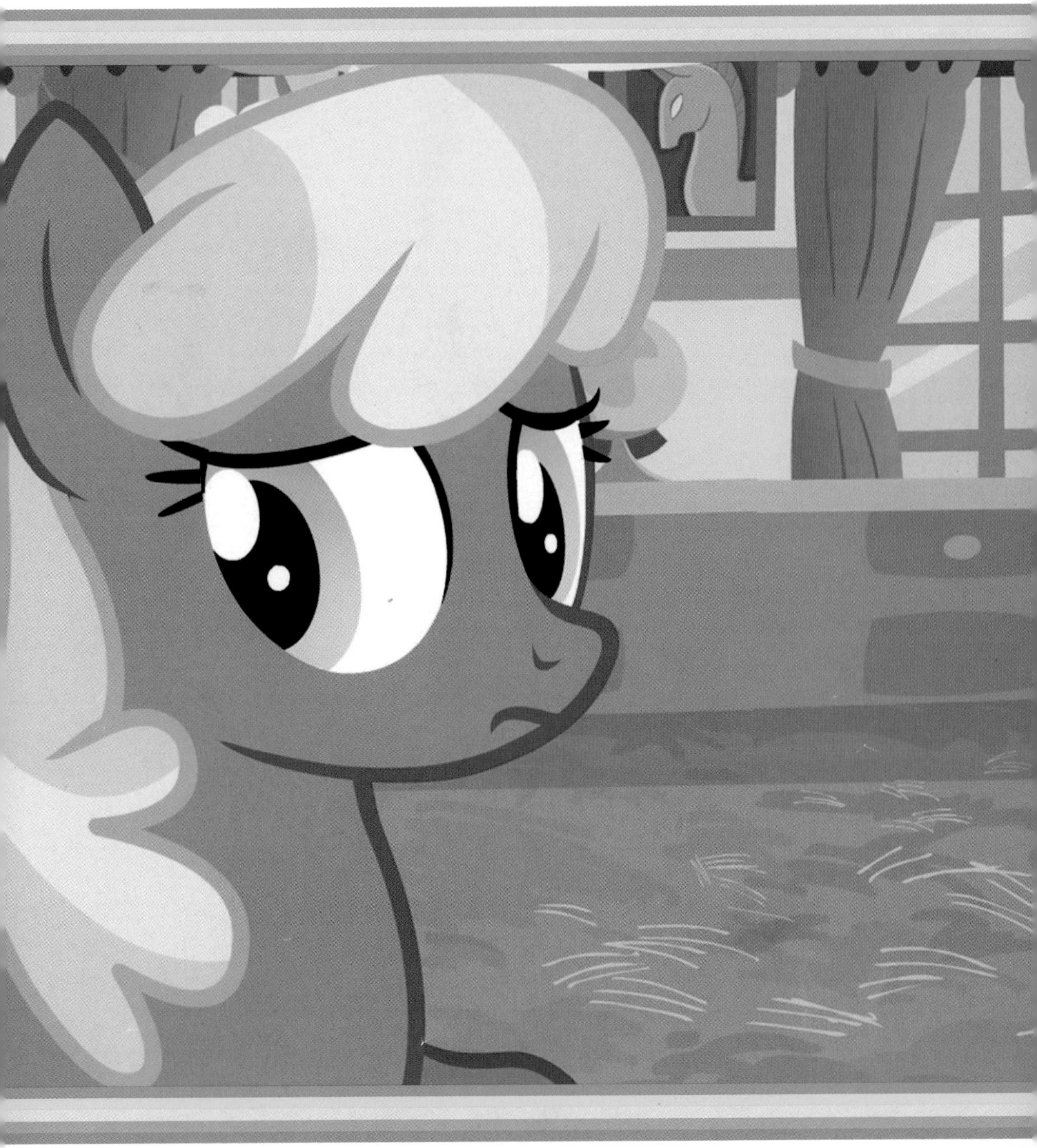

"We will find her a special somepony," they say.

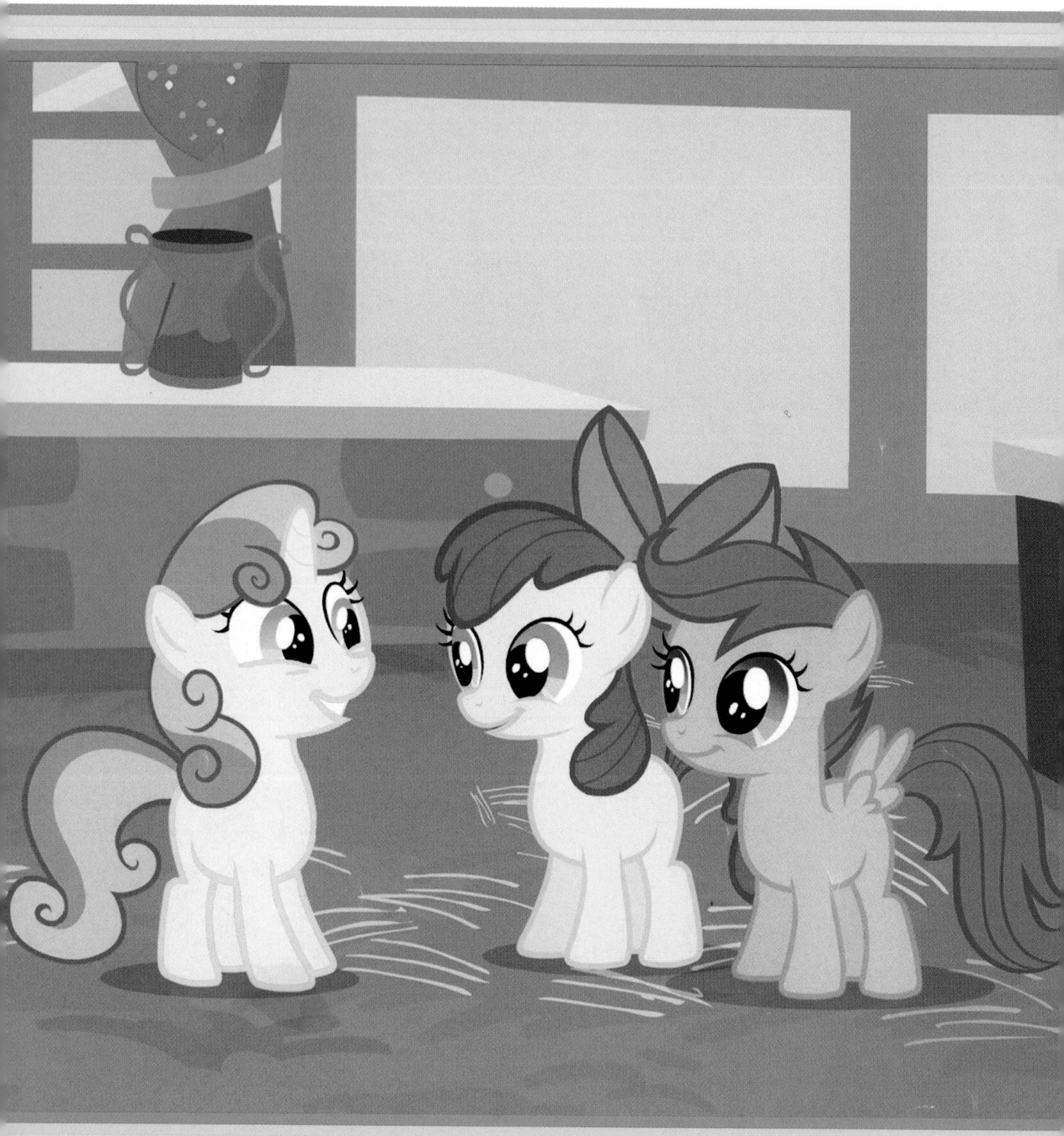

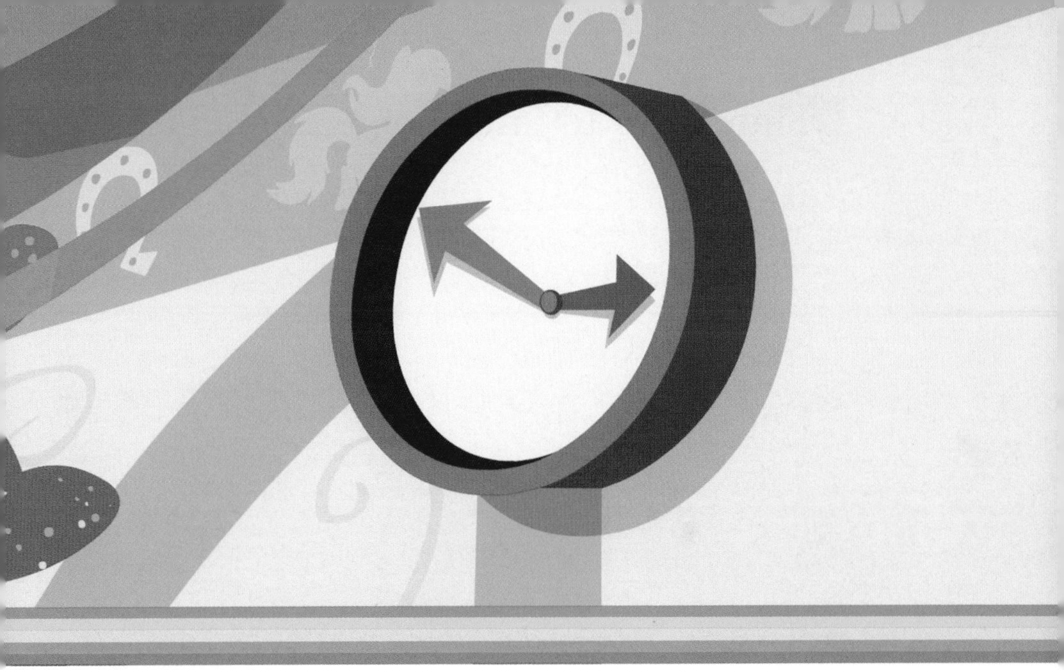

They do not have much time.
Hearts and Hooves Day
is almost over.

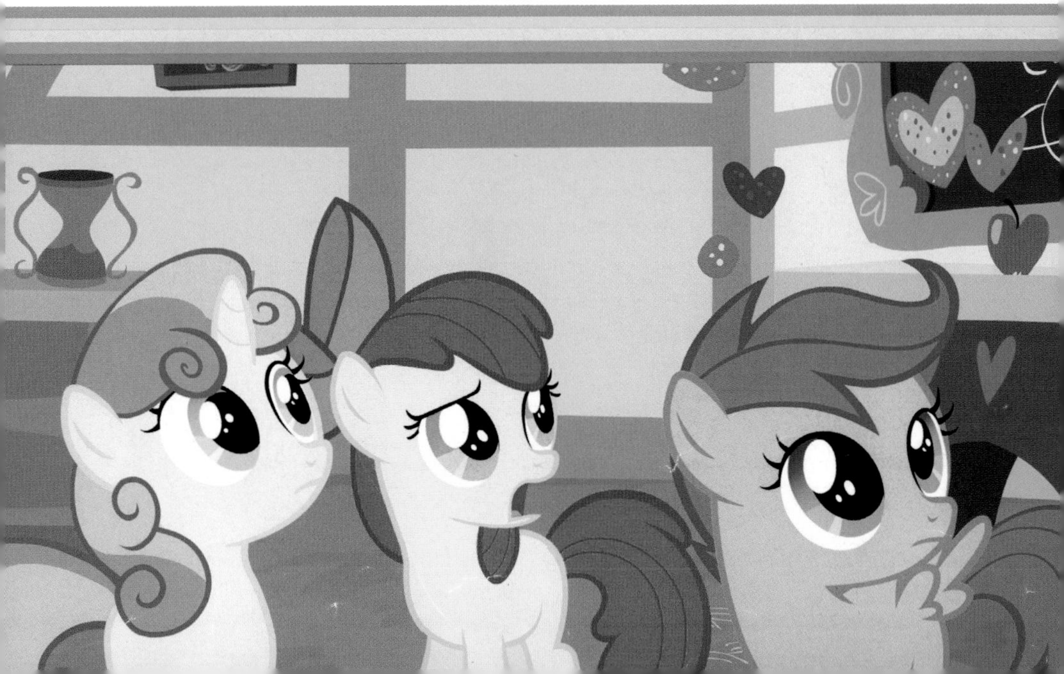

They have to find the perfect
stallion for Miss Cheerilee.
Not too silly.
Not too flashy.
Not too smelly.

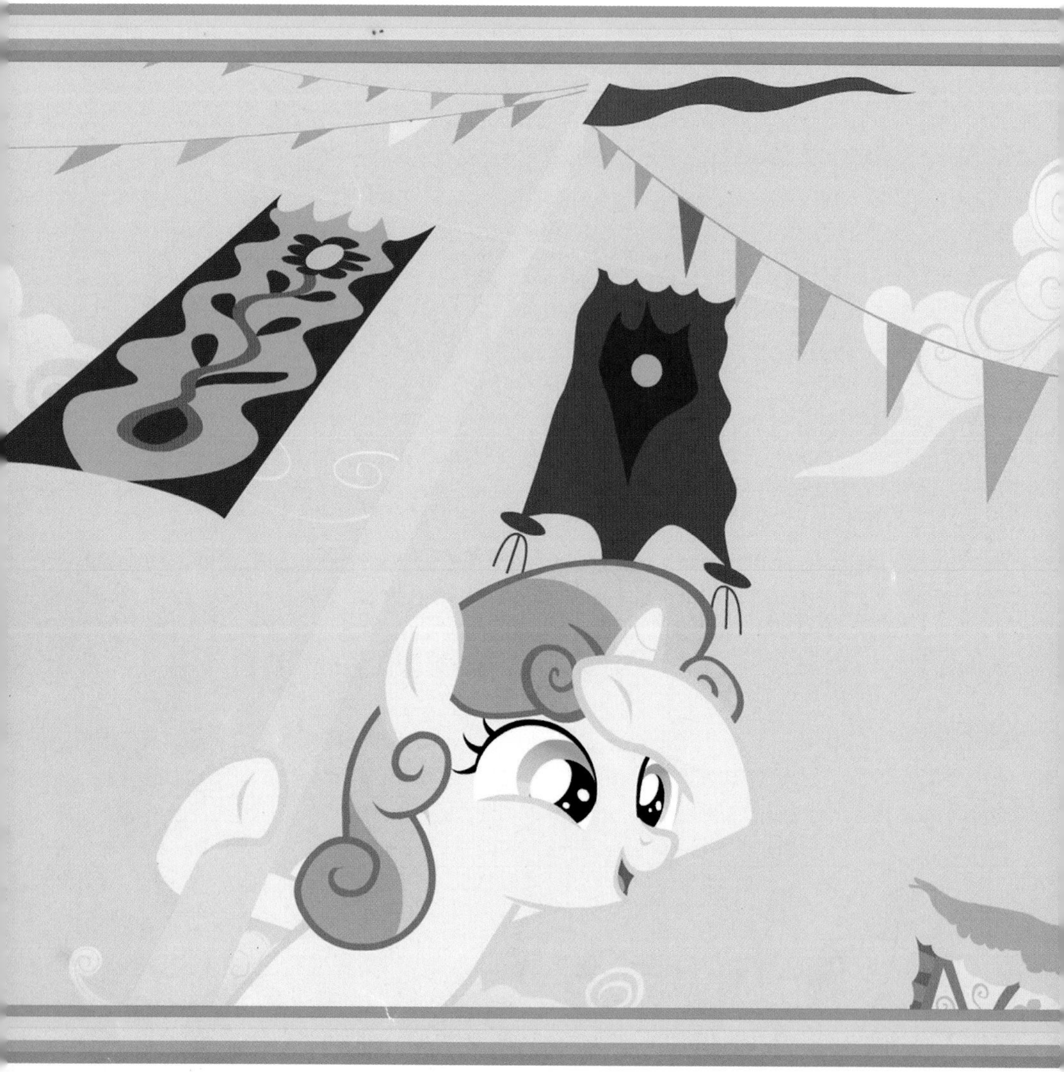

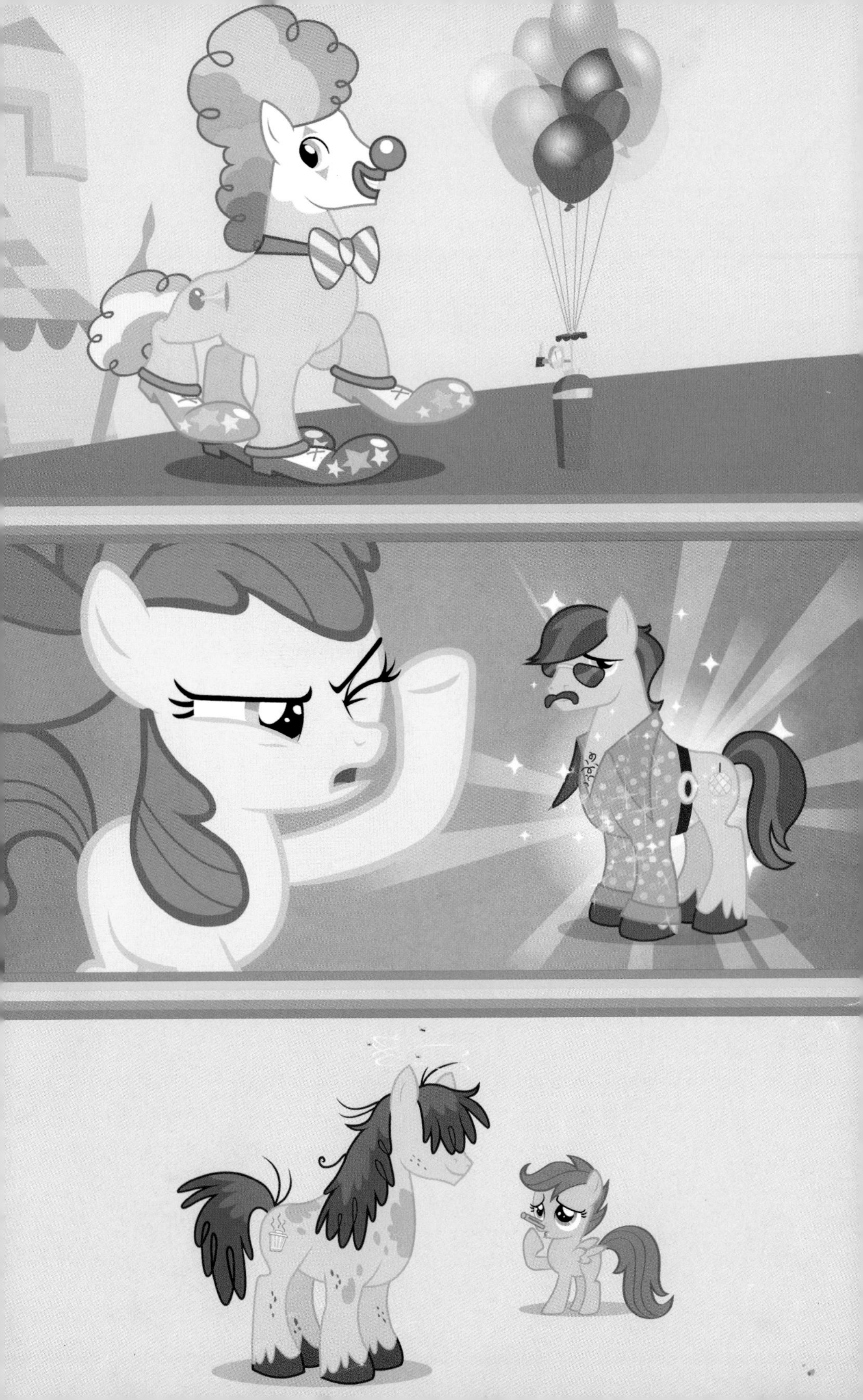

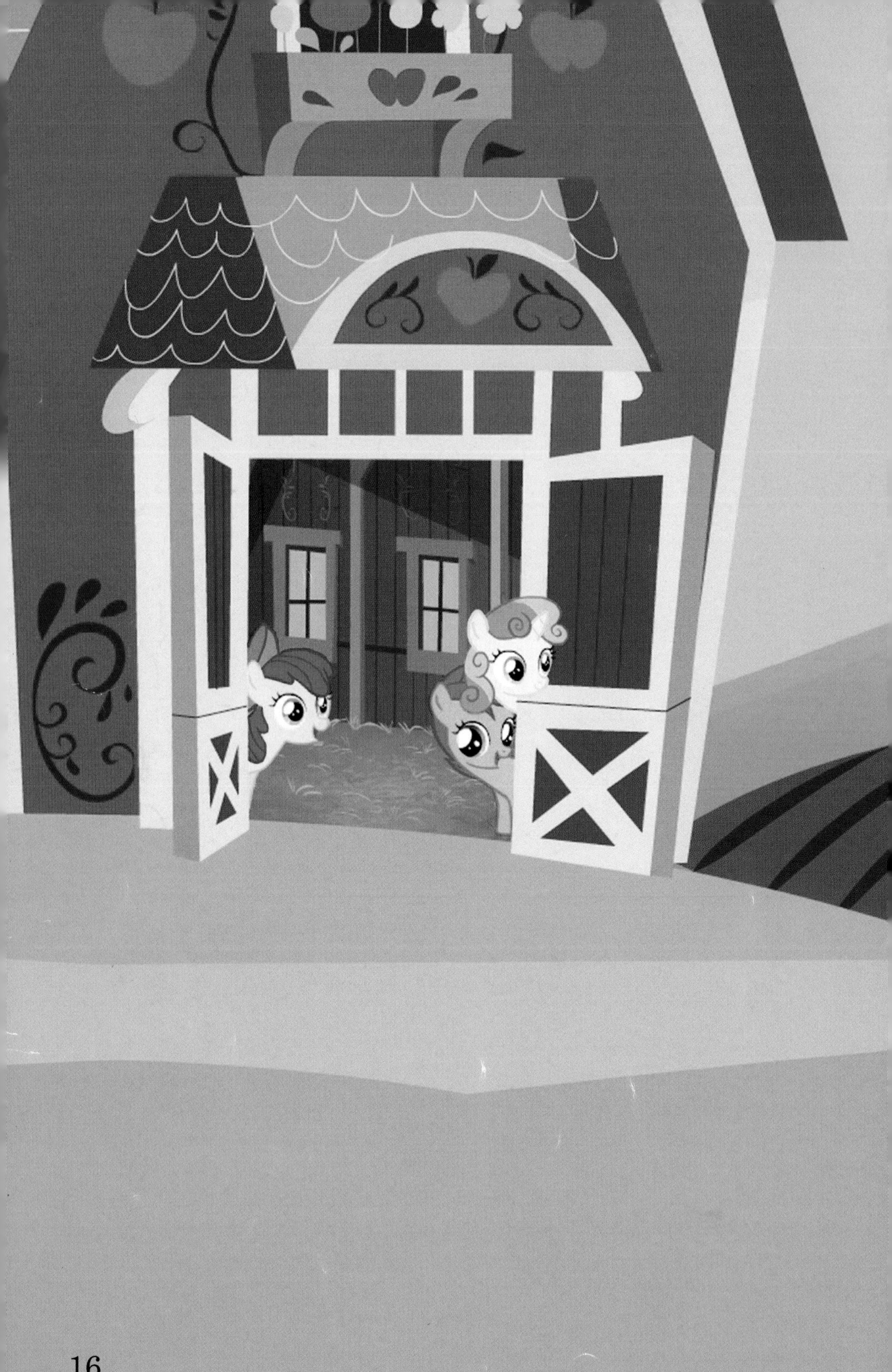

"He is the one!" says Scootaloo.
She nods at Big McIntosh.
"My brother?" asks Apple Bloom.

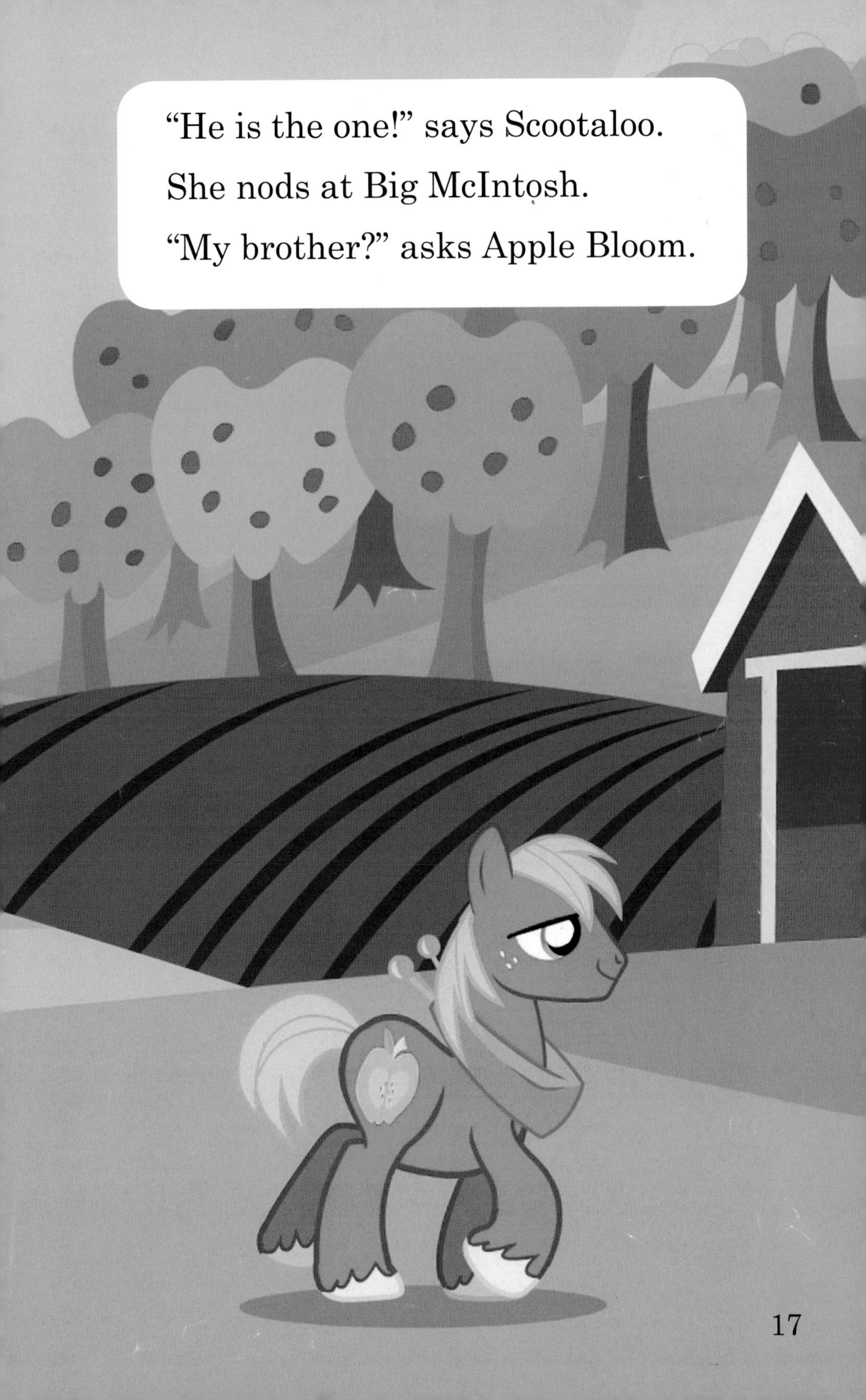

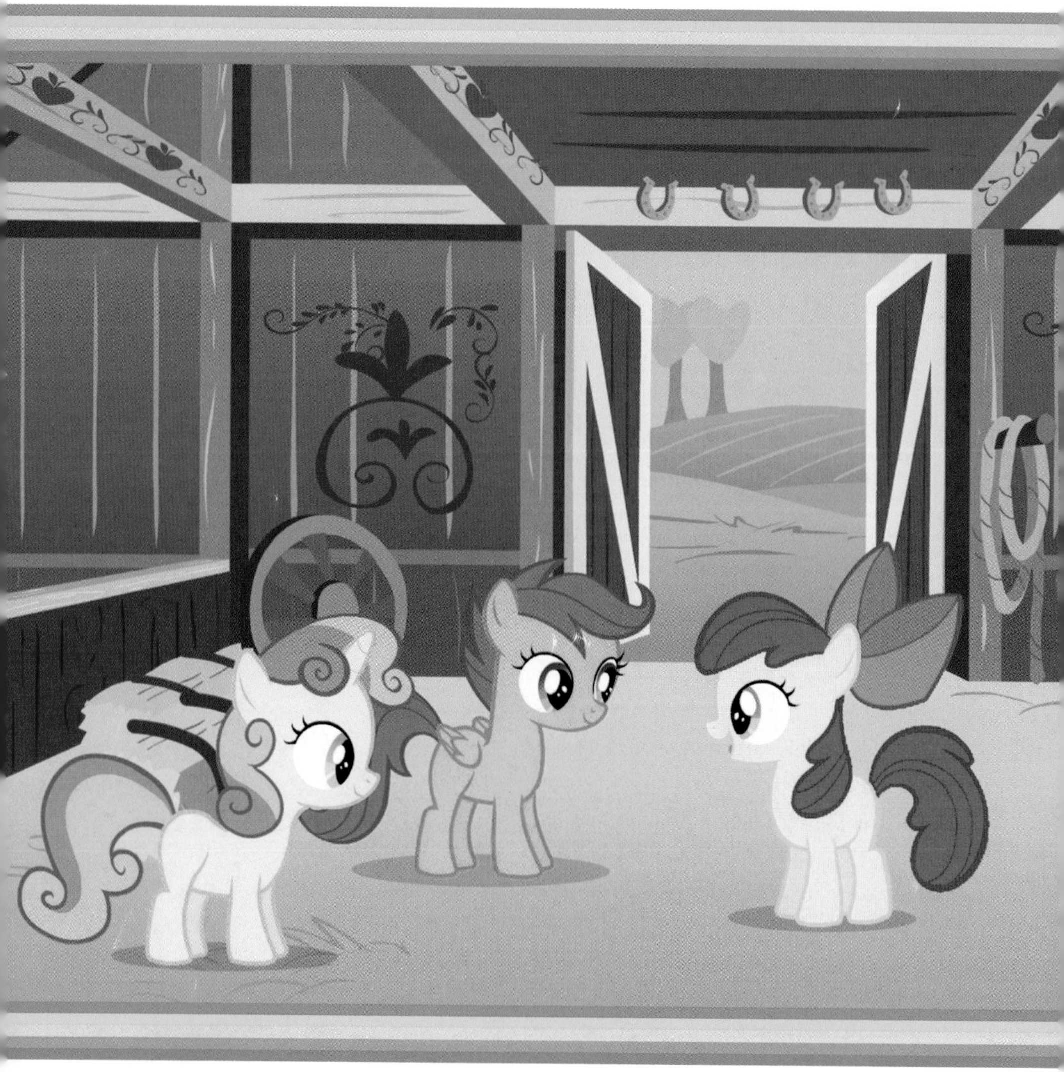

"Big Mac is nice,
and he works hard,"
says Scootaloo.
"They will fall in love,"
says Apple Bloom.

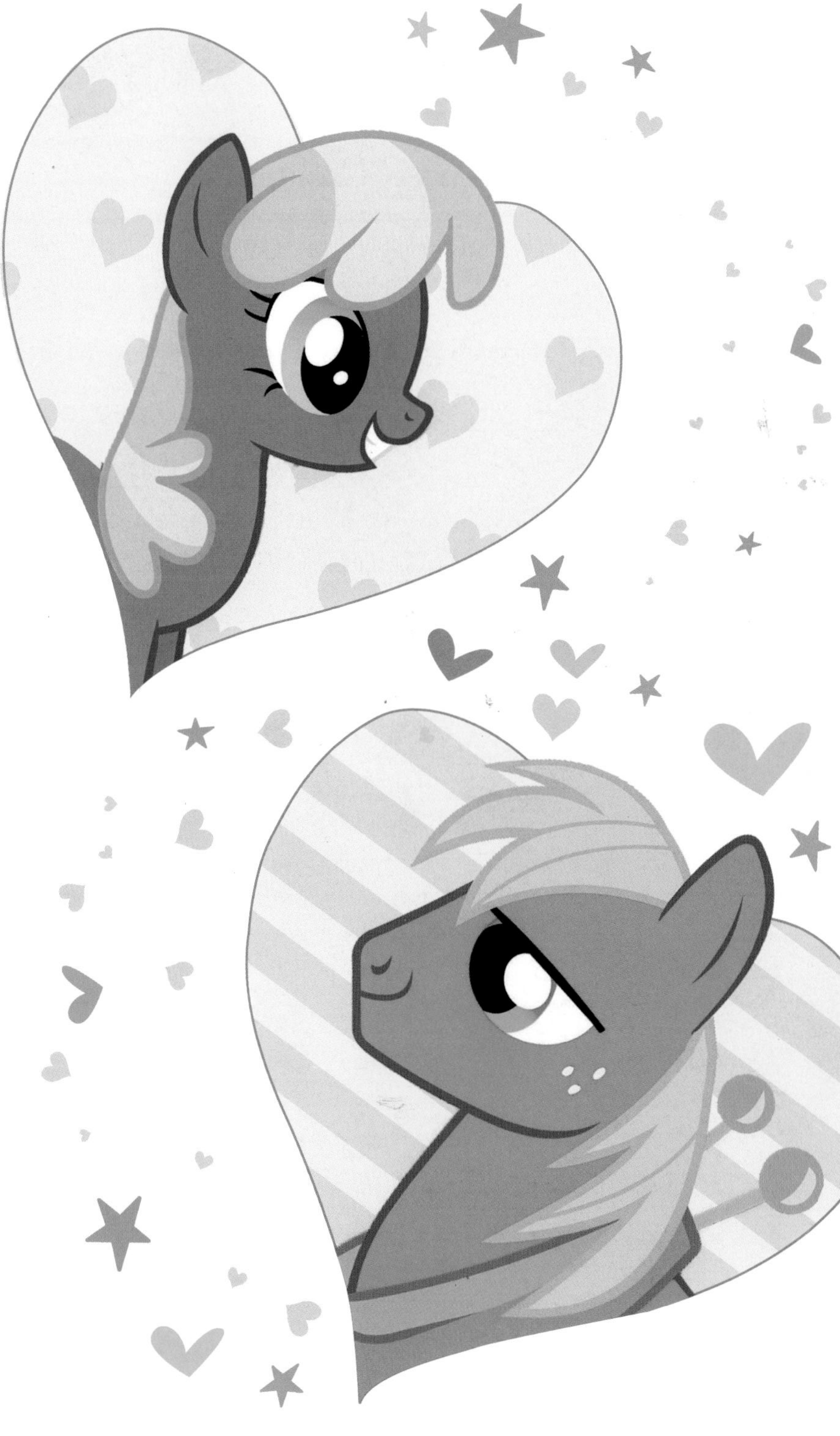

The Cutie Mark Crusaders
set up a picnic date for
Big Mac and Miss Cheerilee.
But they do not fall in love.

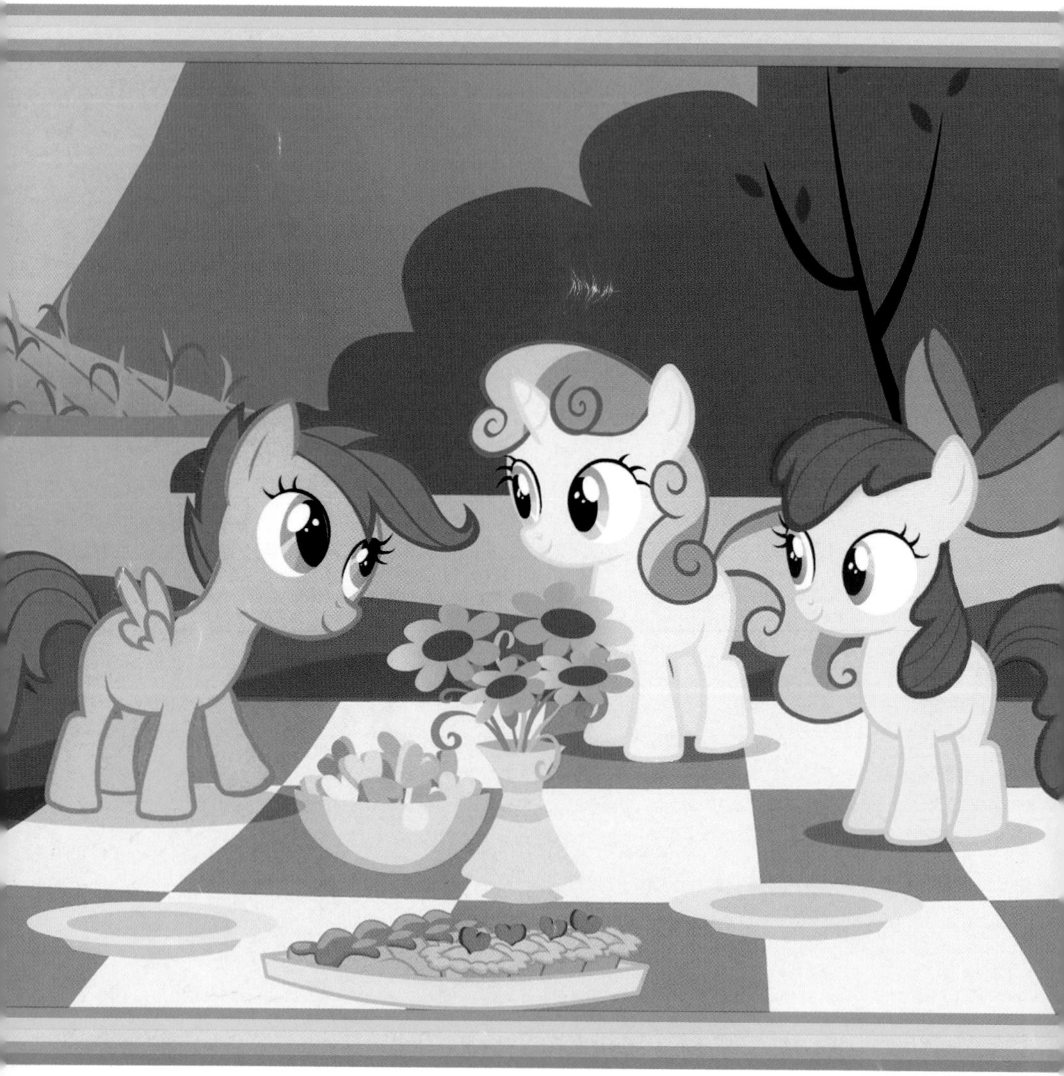

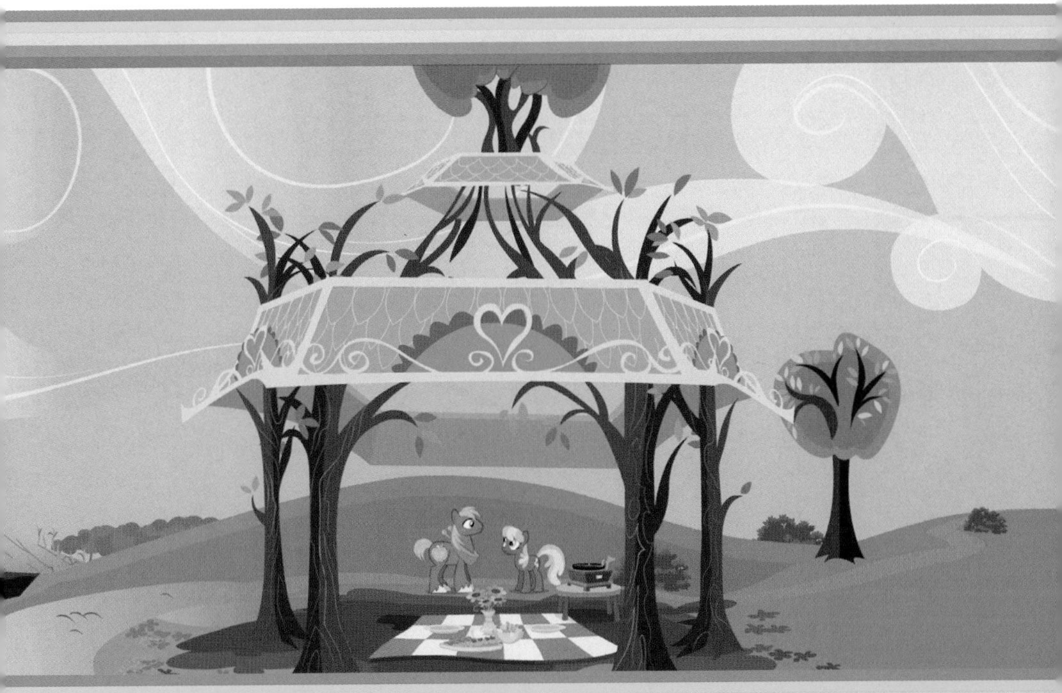

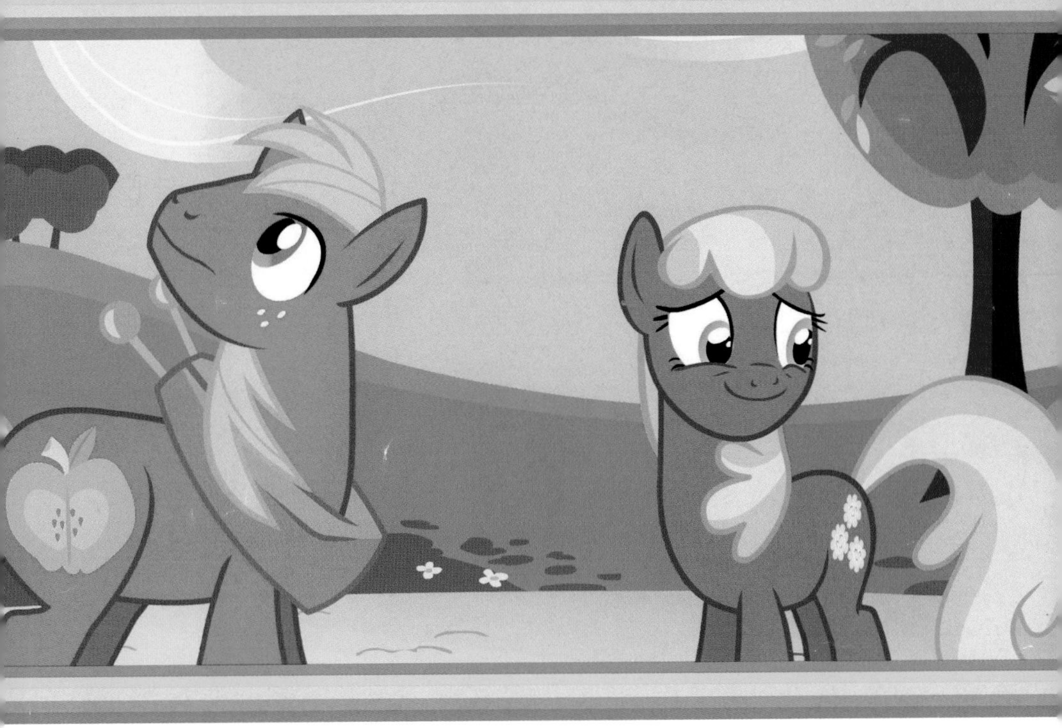

Later, the ponies see
Twilight Sparkle.
She has a book
about love potions.
It gives them a new idea!

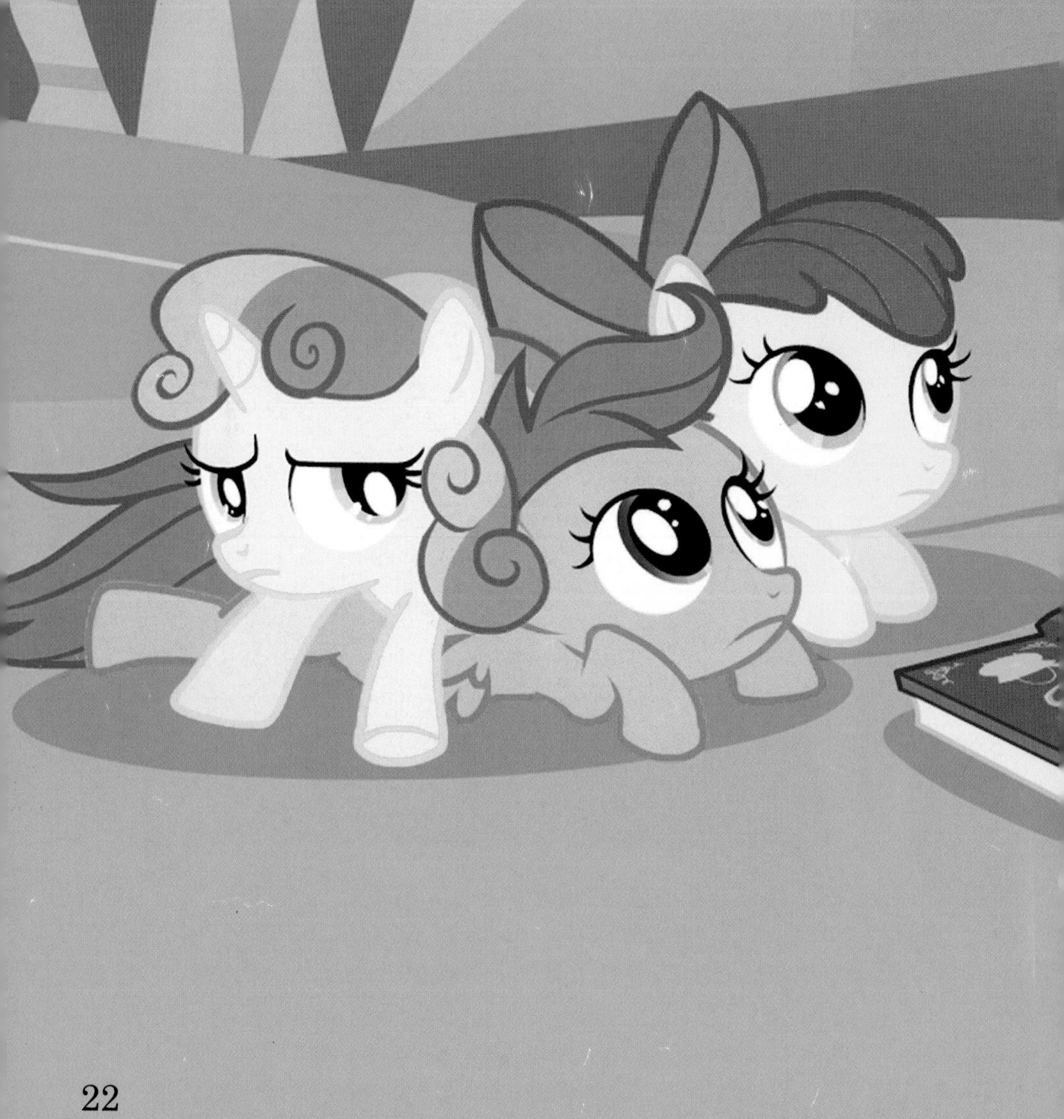

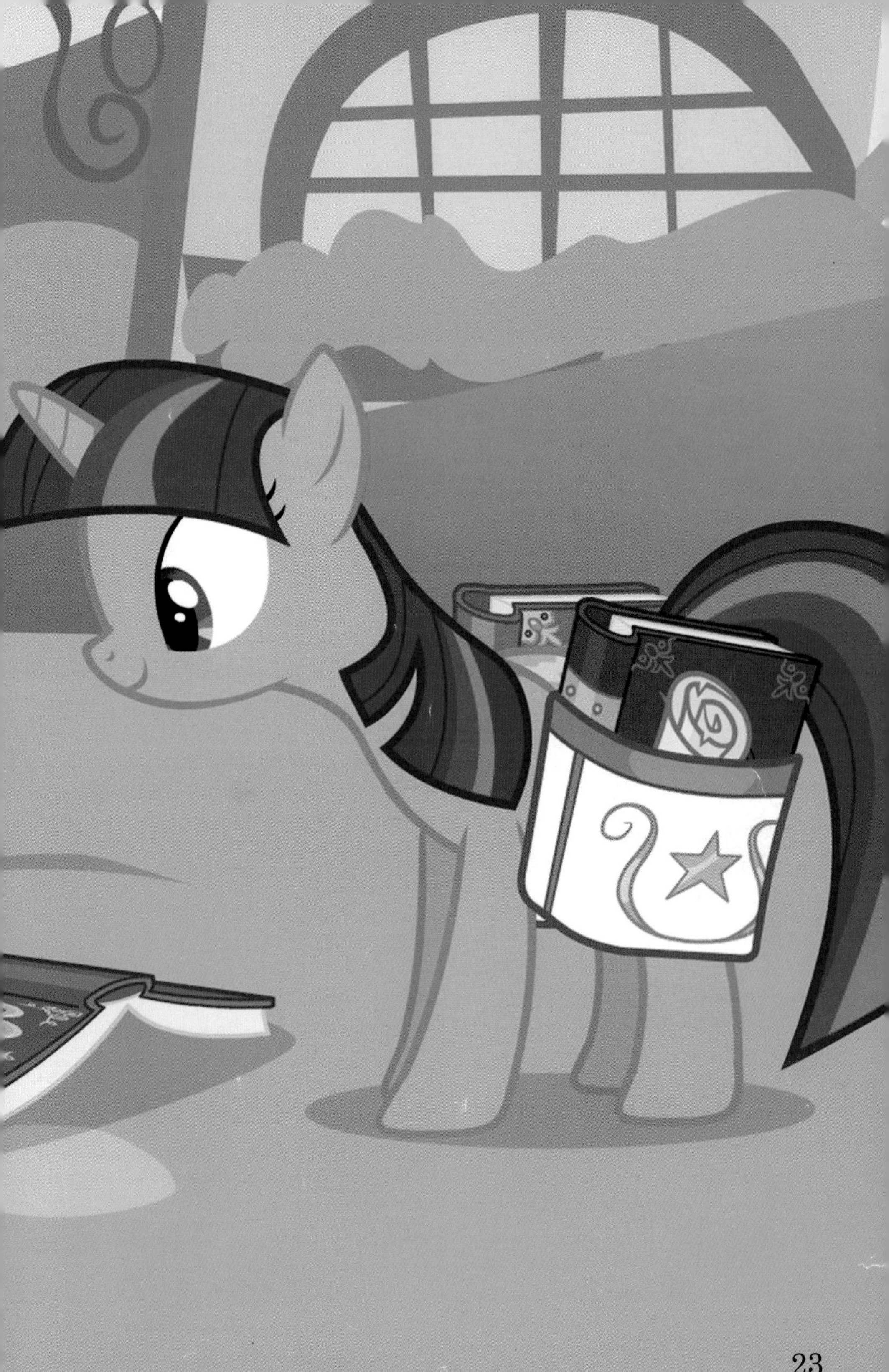

They mix up a love potion
for Big Mac and Miss Cheerilee.

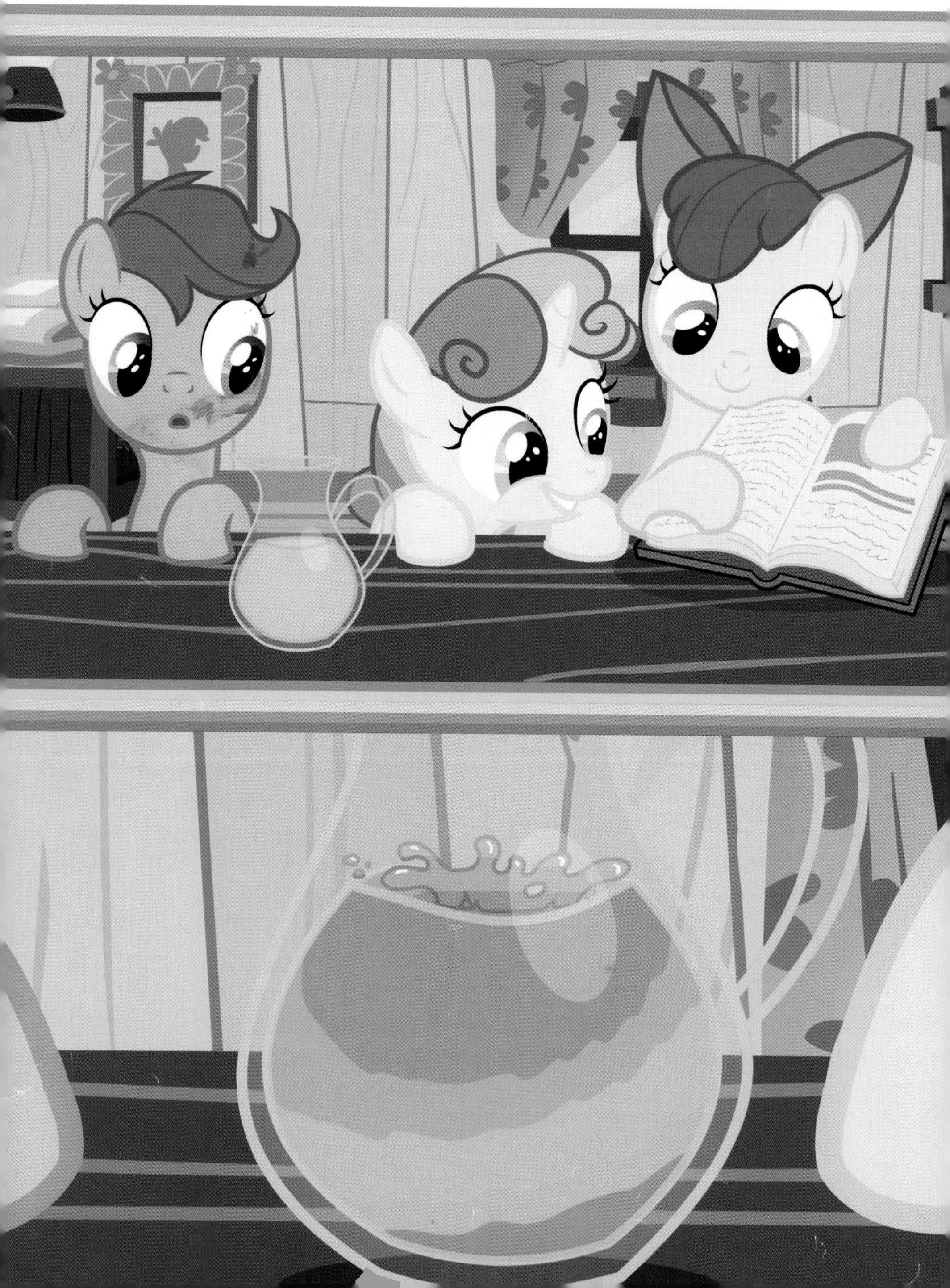

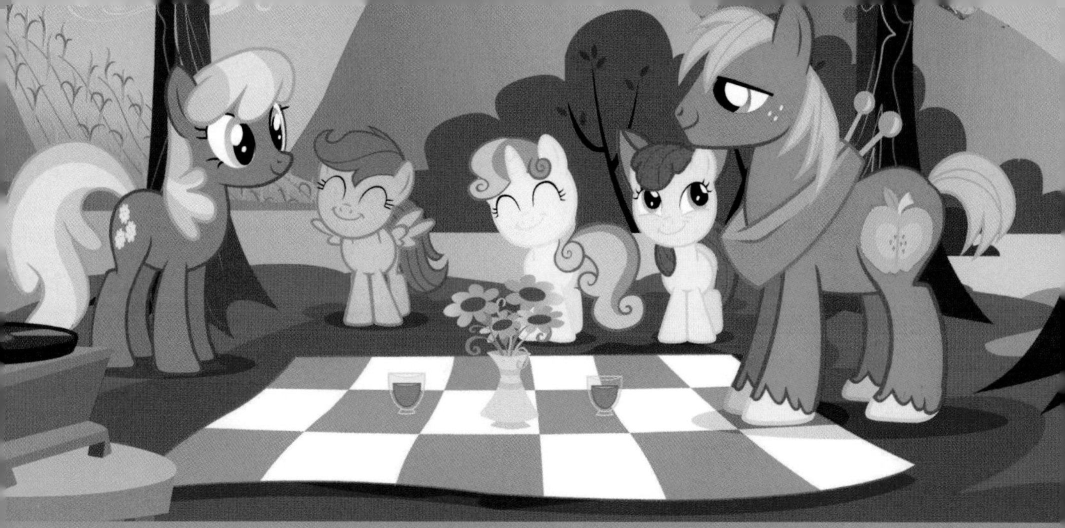

Miss Cheerilee and Big Mac
drink the love potion.

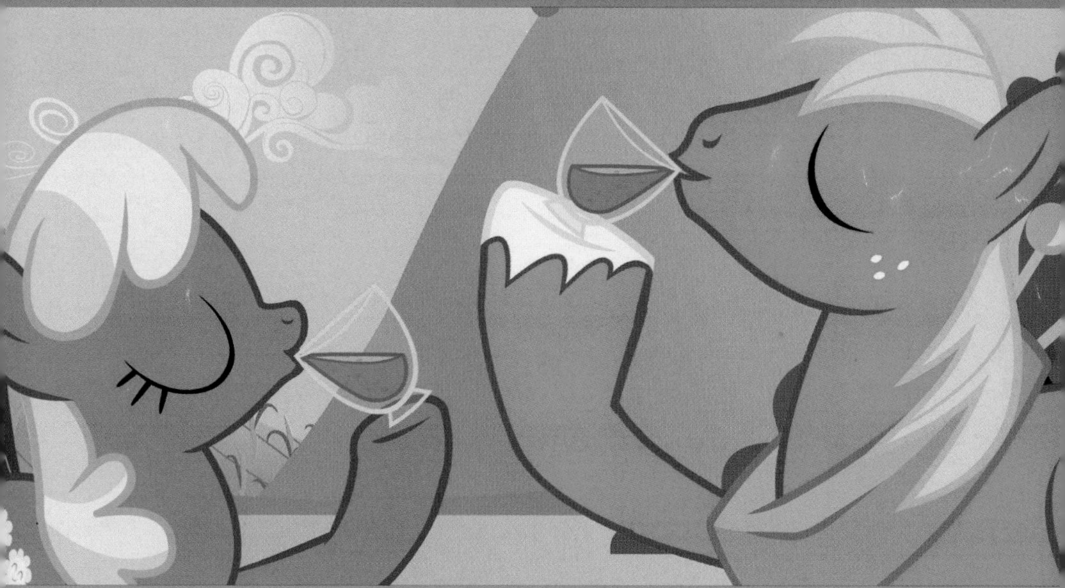

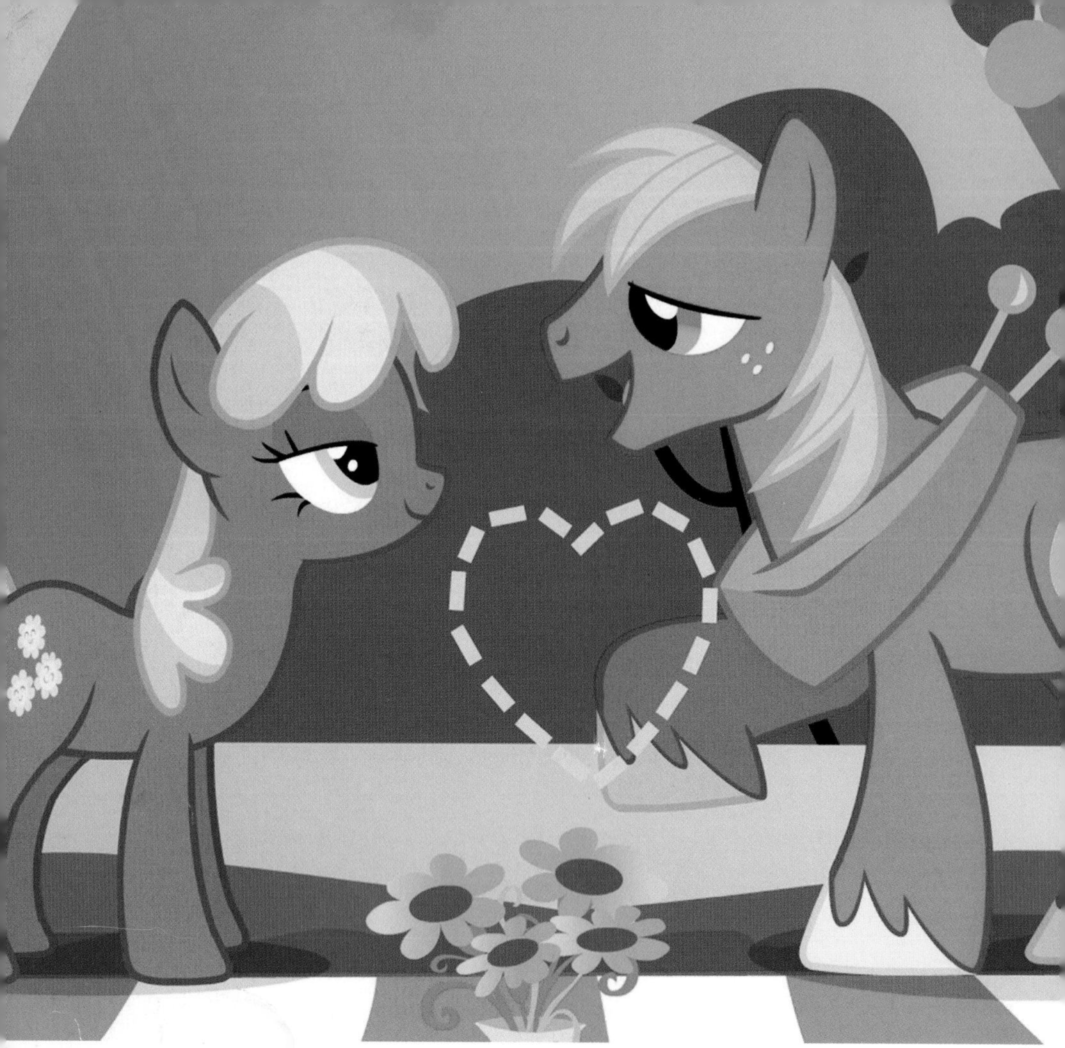

Big Mac and Miss Cheerilee
fall in love right away.
They call each other
silly names like Pony Pie
and Shmoopie Moopie.

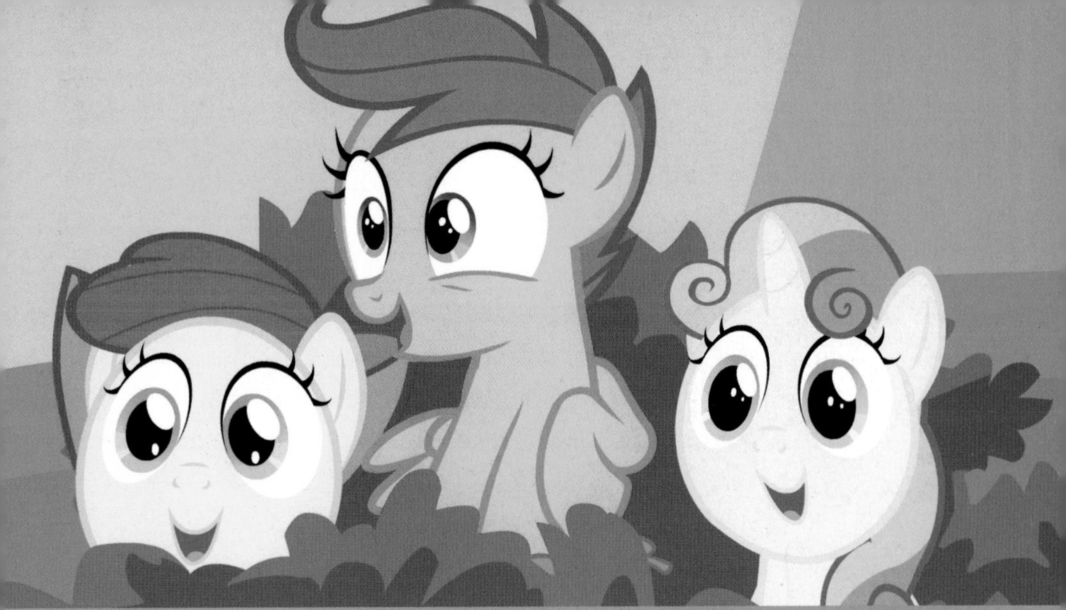

"It worked!" the ponies cheer.

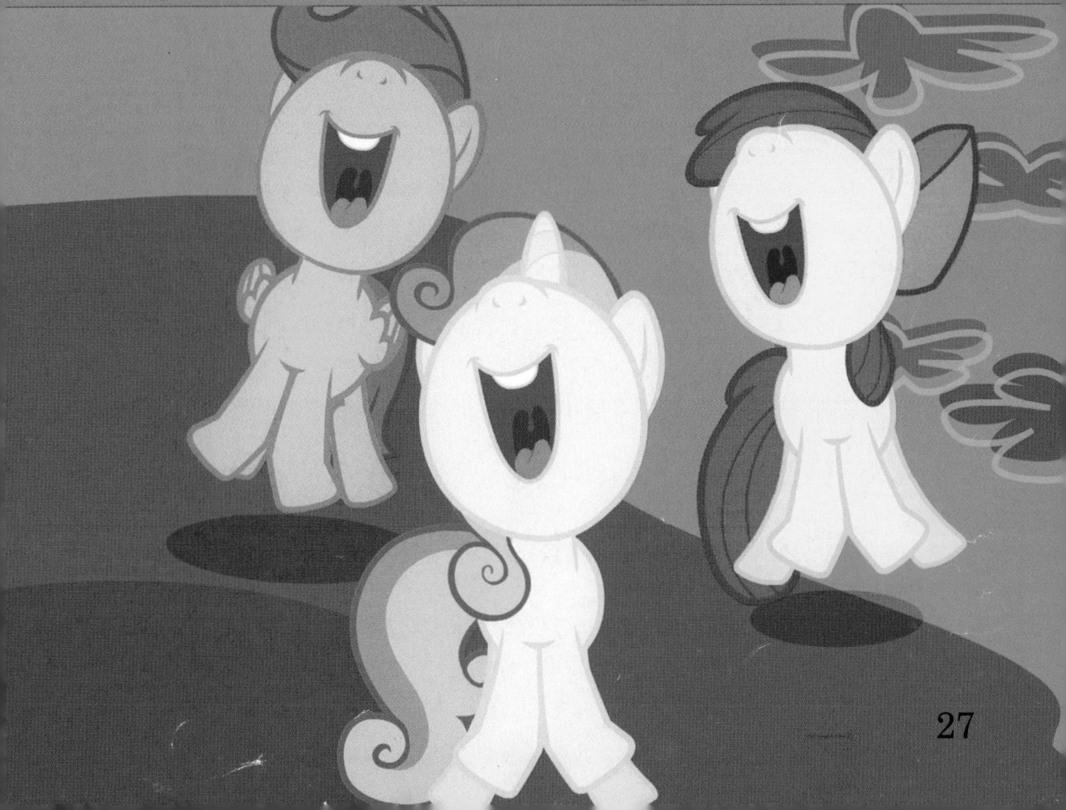

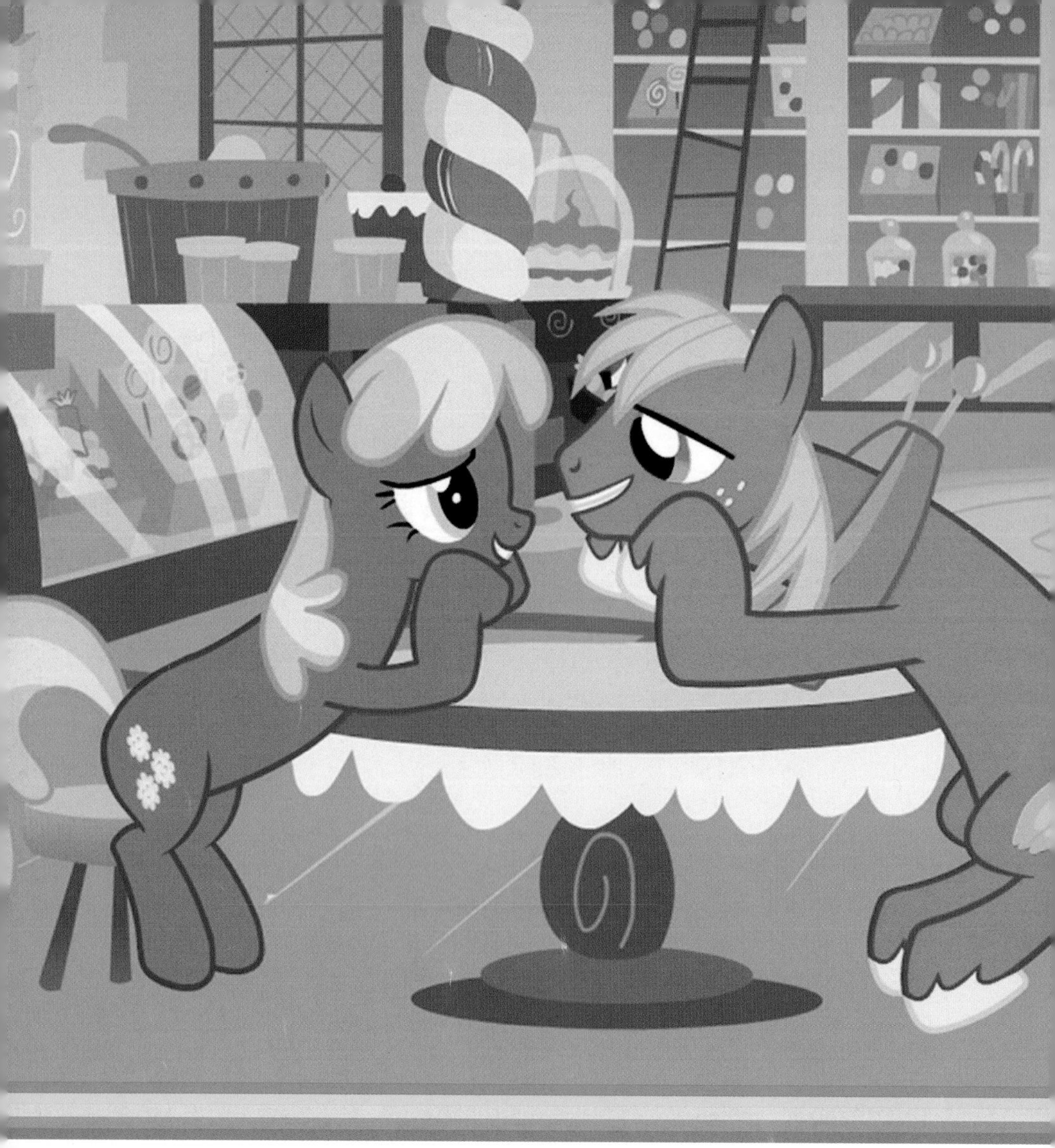

But Big Mac and Miss Cheerilee
are TOO much in love.
They stare at each other all day.
They are not themselves.
They even decide to get married!

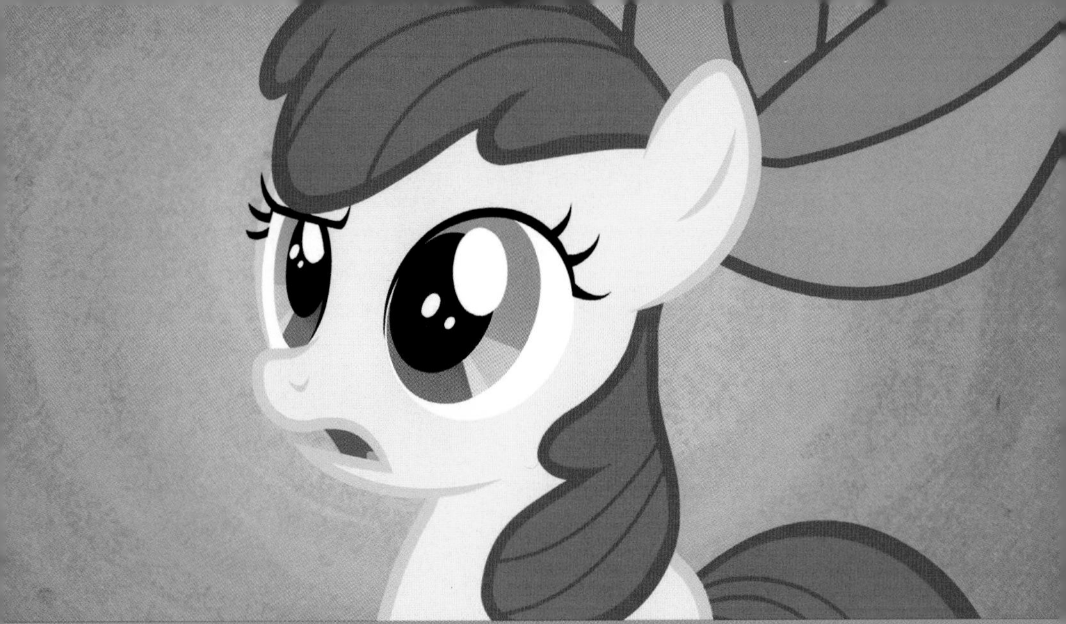

"We made a mistake,"
says Apple Bloom.
"We need to undo the spell
that the potion put on them."

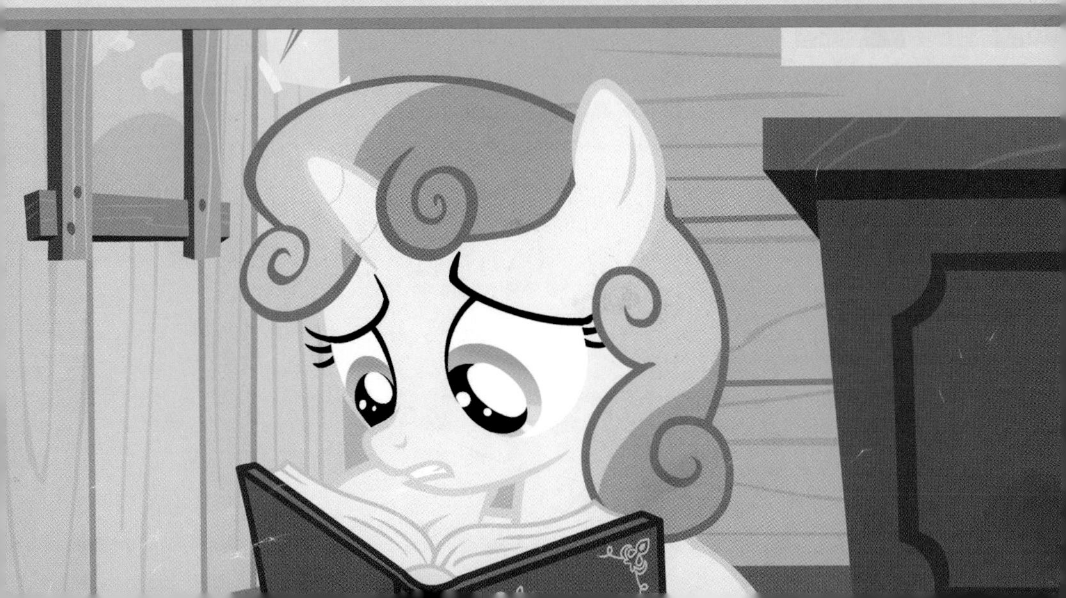

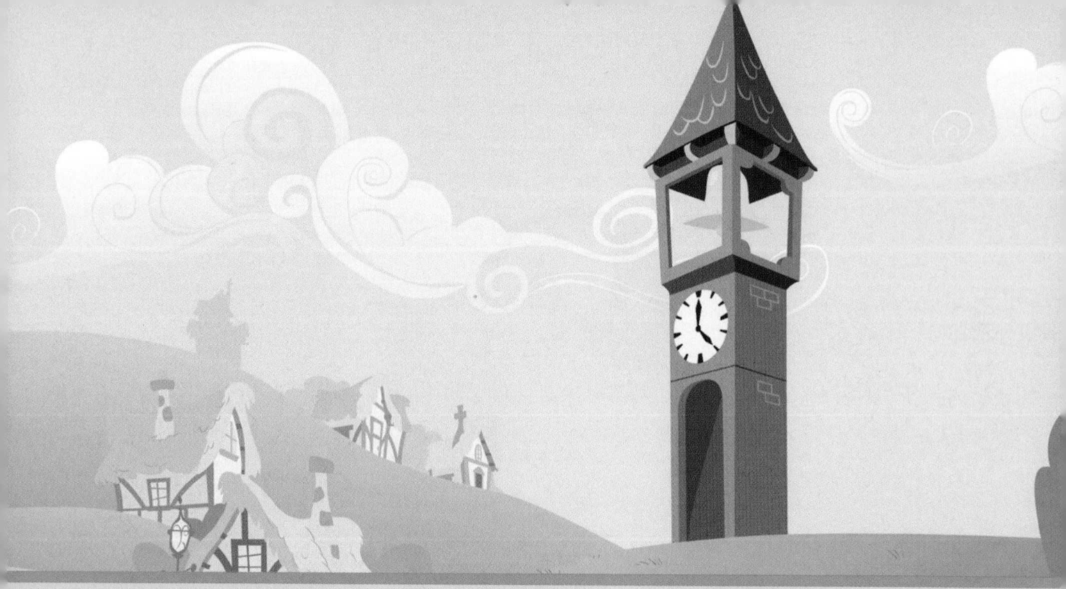

To break the spell, the ponies have to keep Big Mac and Miss Cheerilee apart for one hour. “We should go plan your wedding!” they tell Miss Cheerilee.

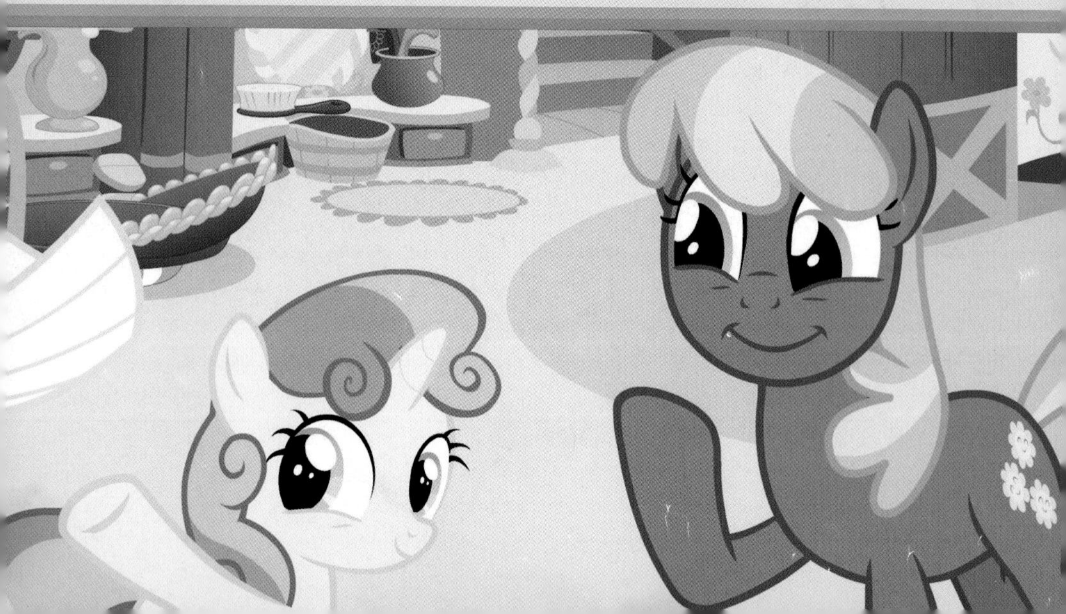

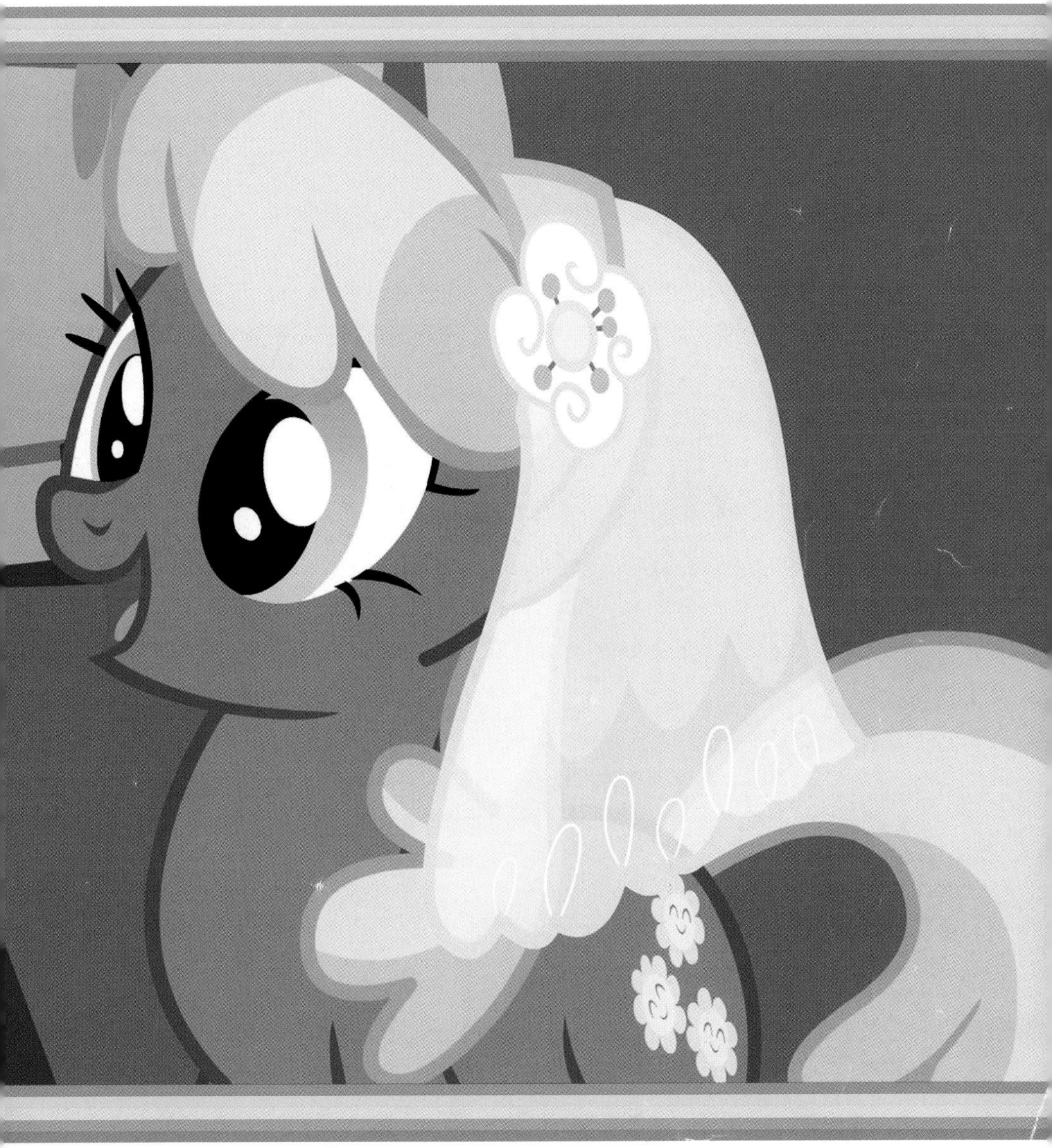

Time passes, and the spell is broken!
Miss Cheerilee and Big Mac
are back to normal.
"I hope you have learned something.
Everypony has to find their own special
somepony," says Miss Cheerilee.

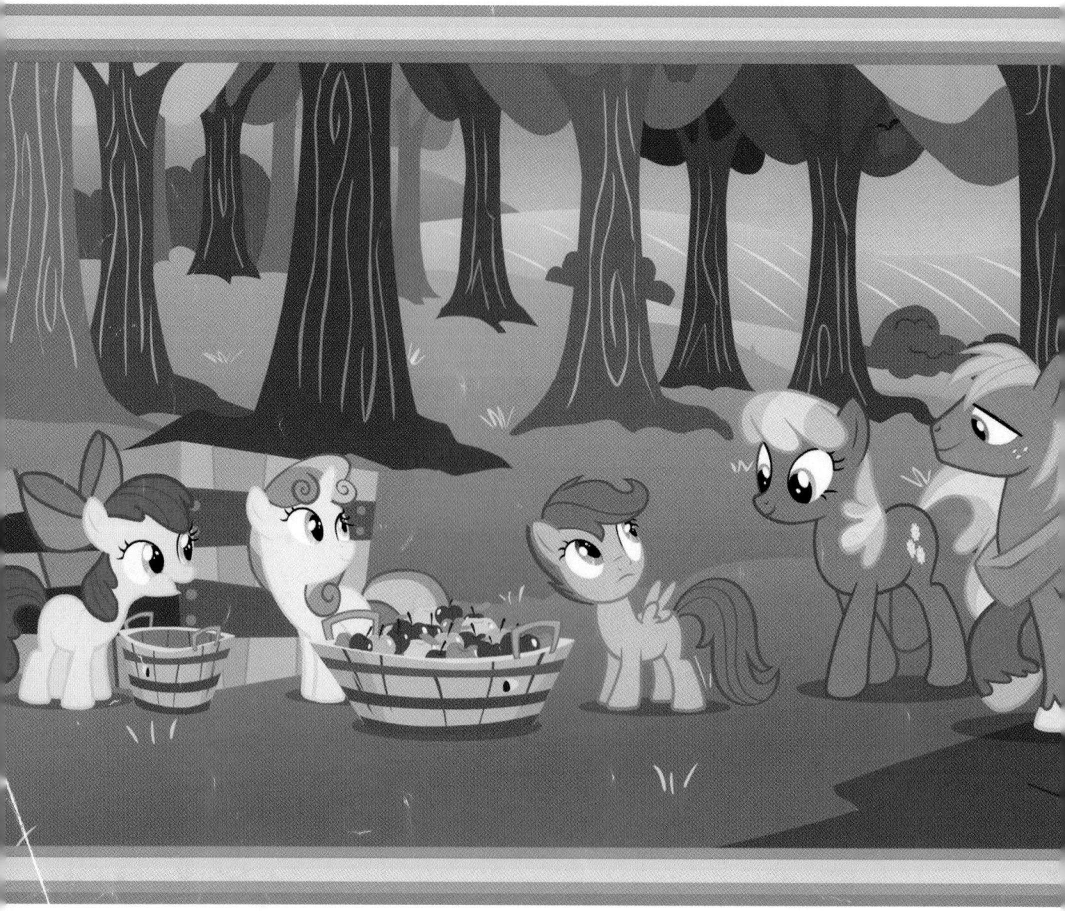

31901061101905